The Lizard Club

NEW AUTONOMY SERIES
Jim Fleming & Peter Lamborn Wilson, Editors

The Lizard Club

Steve Abbott

Autonomedia

Acknowledgements

The interviews with Jerome Caja (Chapter 3) and Sean SP (Chapter 10) were originally published in *The Bay Area Reporter*. A version of the "Hippie Histomap" (Chapter 4) appeared in the last issue of *Homocore*. Chapter 5 collapses together two of my columns from the *San Francisco Sentinel*. Chapter 6 first appeared in *Holy Tit Clamps* #9. I wrote Chapter 8 collaboratively with Lex Lonehood. Chapter 14 was included in the anthology *Discontents*, edited by Dennis Cooper, and Chapter 15 was first published in *PC Casualties* #1. Chapter 18 is a real questionnaire, which I mailed to real people (25 of whom responded), and Chapter 19, by Kevin Killian, includes a letter he really wrote and sent to Whitley Streiber.

For a list of the titles drawn upon to compose Chapter 21, please send a SASE to *Lizard List* care of Autonomedia, below. Since I have stolen so many sentences from others, I can't very well complain if others steal from me. "All property is theft."

Special thanks to Hakim Bey, Jim Fleming and Dave Mandl.

Design & Text Production: Jordan Zinovich
Author's Photo: Stan J. Maletic

Autonomedia
POB 568 Williamsburgh Station
Brooklyn, New York 11211-0568 USA

718-387-6471

Printed in the United States of America

CONTENTS

–1–

WAKING UP

I'm in bed with a friend, not for sex, but to keep warm in the cold room. He's curled against the wall grasping most of the sheet and flimsy green thermal blanket which I'm trying to get my legs under. The phone by the bed rings, various guys I don't know wanting to come over. "Oh, he's so and so's lover," D. says when I tell him the last caller's name. Actually D. says a name like Scott or David, which I don't recall.

At some point, because of the phone calls, I begin to realize people are coming from all over the world to hear John Waters give a lecture in our apartment. Quick images: me in the kitchen asking Waters to autograph my birth certificate; me asking if he's ever met Kenneth Anger and, if so, what he's like. (This last is a zoom revealing a nervous twitch around John's mouth. Then a reverse zoom, John talking to an overflow crowd in our living room.)

"Everybody loves a theory," John drones. He points to an oval mirror into which Kenneth Anger is escaping. Waters looks at me and winks.

I wake up. It's dark. Slowly I peel myself away from the dream and hold it up in my mind like a suit of skin. It's happy, unlike yesterday's about my ex. I shut my eyes again to savor the warmth of the covers I've finally gotten under, but no more pleasant images jump to life beneath my eyelids; instead, below, I feel a nagging pressure—my bladder.

I get up and stumble down the hall into the bathroom. Flip switch. The brightness of the narrow room makes me wince. I pull myself into focus by staring into the toilet bowl. Tiny bubbles form, then drift outward, from the point at which my urine hits water. Some bubbles pop but more are formed until three quarters of the water is covered. When my pee stops most of the bubbles pop, except for three shrinking islands which rotate slowly in the pale yellow water until they too disappear. I reach over to the chrome handle protruding from the toilet tank and flush, then I wish I hadn't because the noise might wake A. who has a virus, hives all over her face and neck. "I wish it was Halloween," A. said last night. "Then I could go outside and scare someone."

Back in my room I fold my futon, dress, and return to the bathroom to shave. The face in the mirror stares at me coldly. Once I looked into its eyes and said, "Steve, I really love you." The face lit up in a grin so disarming that I laughed and at the same time thought, "Boy are you crazy."

I glance through the morning paper as I gulp down vitamins and juice. *The Far Side* shows a balloon-headed kid. "C'mon Dad! Shoot the apple! Shoot the apple!" he says, and the caption reads: "William Tell's older, less fortunate son." I tear out the cartoon, fold it in half, and put it in my billfold. Then I walk downstairs, cross street to the bus stop, and look at a display window full of comics while I wait: *Flash Gordon Meets the Lizard Men*, *Teenage Mutant Ninja Turtles*, *The Green Hornet vs. Dr. Strange*. The bus arrives. I get on.

I get off at Van Ness and Market and run down the

escalator two steps at a time to the underground which is faster. I zip around commuters in suits and ties. A few minutes later I notice a young Asian who was also on the bus opening a larger-than-usual-size paperback: Bram Stoker's *Dracula*. My estimation of him rises. "Is that good?" I wanna ask, but can't think how to say this without sounding corny. What I really want to ask is, "Can I take off your clothes and put your body in my mouth?" but an L arrives. I'm sucked in like a crumpled cigarette pack pulled into a drain by the combined forces of gravity and a swirling surge of rainwater.

Two inches from my face, the red neck of a man whose hair is growing over the boundary of last week's razorline haircut. He's got a pinkish white spot on his neck as if he had a thumbtack stuck there while he was getting his tan. Musta fallen off—the thumbtack I mean.

Turning away I see a hand gripping a vertical metal pole. On its wrist a dark blue plastic watchband holds a conceptual art watch. No numbers, just geometric shapes: a yellow triangle, two red rectangles, a couple of green squares. Innumerable light brown hairs push every which way over the watchband, like magnified insect hairs. It's a landscape of bumps, craters, and hairs blowing like pampas grass in the slight breeze from an air duct overhead.

I turn my head slightly left. On the other side of the hand, a young man with a thin face and neatly combed hair stares out the window. He comes in and out of view as the car lurches. His pale skin glows. No hairs, moles, or blemishes. In his reflection against the darkened glass I see the other side of his face. It's more ominous, an evil twin. When next I glimpse the young man I notice his lips are too thick, and his jaw is too long to go with his pinched nose. This anomaly stirs my interest. I shift my weight from foot to

9

foot. We disembark at Montgomery, walking in opposite directions.

Following sixty or so pairs of legs up the escalator, I pass nine newspaper boxes, two traffic lights, three liquor stores, the Venus Cafe, several Chinese luncheonettes, two computer stores, and three stores selling office supplies, until I see my own reflection in the thick plate glass doors of 440 - 2nd Street.

Pushing the right door's polished brass handle I walk across a blue-tiled floor, barely glancing to the right at the law office where, through more glass, one can see a plump receptionist and, sitting on the white counter in front of her, four birds-of-paradise in a pink and grey vase. The elevator doors stand open at the far end of the lobby. The elevator has grey carpeted walls and a computerized light that announces your floor. I walk in and press button number five. The doors shut and the elevator starts to rise.

When the computerized light announces five, the elevator stops and I step out. I turn left and walk down the hall to The Research Spectacle, where Murr, a twenty-five-year-old New Wave male secretary, greets me by saying: "Hey, hey, whadaya say Kiiiiiiid-dough!"

Murr grins euphorically, the way a retarded child or speed freak might. No one who works here looks unhappy, because if you do you get fired.

"Hi Murr," I say, putting on my happiest face.

On the white wall next to Murr's desk hangs a Warhol print of pink and yellow flowers. Behind him stretches a row of white cubicles. Newly painted grey beams jut from the ceiling to the grey carpeted floor at forty five degree angles.

As I walk down the hallway I hear fashionably dressed young women talking into sleek white telephones. Actually, they're not telephones but computers that make seven varieties of melodious beeps. A new employee needs two days to learn how to operate one.

When I get to the end of the hall, I turn right and walk to the coffee machine. Next to the coffee machine is the employee bulletin board. I pin up my cartoon of William Tell's older, less fortunate son. Then I pour some coffee into a styrofoam cup, drop in a cube of C & S sugar, and stir in a spoonful of Cremora. Armed with my coffee I pivot right and walk down to the coding room, where I slide into an orange plastic chair in front of a long brown formica table.

"Coffee?"

Since quitting smoking, my left ear is plugged with mucus. I think my co-worker Jim has asked for a copy. But of what? Tally sheets? When I ask, Jim laughs. He can't hear so well himself because he's wearing radio headphones.

I reach for a stack of twenty-five Tell-A-Friend computer questionnaires. When I have a stack in front of me I feel secure. Coding is as tranquil as listening to Philip Glass.

The occupation code, which I do first, is easy unless you have to search pages of small print to see if an enlisted military person goes under "7," service worker, or "5" unskilled worker. Pilots and officers go under "1," professionals. Later I'll do the Open Ends, questions that seem complicated but actually aren't once you get the hang of it. For instance, in answering "How would you describe the American Dream?" most respondents will write about a) sex, b) money, c) freedom, or d) religious values. If they write anything else, you write "e," other, and list their answers on a separate sheet. Unless they don't answer the question at all, that is, in which case you write "y."

Helga, my new German co-worker, thinks it's stupid to write "y" over and over all day. I agree but say it beats most ways of earning five dollars an hour. (Actually I earn seven dollars, since I've been here the longest. But why emphasize inequality?)

At ten o'clock Maddy walks in, not the balding New Wave secretary but my coding co-worker with long, lustrous reddish-brown hair.

"It's henna," Maddy says when I compliment her. She gives off a pleased little laugh like the sound of a kitten's purr. "In L.A. lots of people's hair bleaches out like this naturally—if they hang out at the beach enough anyway."

Maddy's communist politics give her laugh and nurturing personality an edge. She tells me that her boyfriend Tom, who's in recovery, seems to be getting more fanatical about not wanting to hang around lizards anymore. Maybe it's because he's working in Marin now. Maddy says they stuffed five thousand dollars in one dollar bills into mailers yesterday. The woman whose home they were working in asked Tom to run water for her mother's bath when he went to the bathroom. The steam drove him crazy. I tell Maddy that I used Tom's comment about lizards in my new story. She says it came from Philip K. Dick's biography. I picture Dick's face on the cover, his smile shy and wary like Maddy's, but a bit more arch. Saw it at City Lights last night—the book I mean.

Since I stopped smoking I'm desperate to read. Panic overwhelms me otherwise. Last week I read three Elmore Leonard novels, William Gibson's *Count Zero*, Cook and Kroker's *Excremental Culture and Hyper-Aesthetics*, Jean-Philippe Toussaint's *The Bathroom*, and half of Thomas Bernhard's *Gargoyles*. Leonard's stuff is fast-paced with vivid description but after a while I get a leaden feeling in my guts, not the inspired giddiness I get reading Gibson. The other books were more depressing. Everyone is either sick, stupid, or alienated.

What I really went into City Lights for was something off-beat like Fydor Sologub's *The Petty Demon*, the first

Russian s&m novel about the joys of whipping naked boys. The hero is a wimpy highschool kid whose forty-year-old mistress gets him up in geisha drag for the town ball. Or is it the alcoholic school official, who likes to spank boys but fears his wife's cookbook is a text of black magic? I can't recall. It's getting harder to find good novels than good friends.

Some aisles in City Lights are crowded—can't squeeze anywhere near the 'zine rack—but the clientele is more interesting than elsewhere: old Beats, foreign tourists, young artists. Wish that pale young man in black would approach me, but no, book browsers are as silent as church goers. Looking at him I begin thinking of my favorite Minimal Man song, with its talking intro which begins:

> I hurt all over inside.
> I feel like crying most the time but I... I can't.
> I cry too easily. I can't control it.
> I'm just plain unhappy.
> I've lost interest in everything I used to care about.
> I'm scared as hell.
> I'm bored.
> I can't make decisions.
> I can't concentrate effectively.
> I feel just futile.

Then this droning music begins and the lyrics "Loneliness is a sad place." Wounded boys like this drive me crazy.

To avoid sexual frustration I mull over what I've picked out so far: P.K. Dick's *A Maze of Death*, and a samizdat text: *Nobody, or The Disgospel According to Maria Demnetnay*. I can only afford one. While trying to decide which to buy, I meander into the poetry room and am filled with pleasure to find two of my own books nestled in their alphabetical slots. It's personal invisibility with a modicum of fame, like light French roast coffee with a splash of Amaretto. But where *do* I exist? In the hands of you reading this or...?

"'Y' is for no answer; '1' is for 'nothing,'" I explain to Helga, who's gotten confused again. "You only write '1' if they write the *word* nothing, or 'I'm not interested,' or 'I don't care to sell anything to my friends.' More complicated answers may sometimes be coded A to Z, but in *this* study you write 'e' for anything else and list what they write verbatim on your Others sheet."

Helga still looks confused.

Maddy chimes in about George Grosz and his blasphemy trial. After three years he finally won, but his allegedly obscene drawing was destroyed and he reverted to painting bourgeois landscapes for the rest of his life. The boss comes in.

"Anyone have any questions?"

His glassy eyes glare at us. His pudgy pink jaw juts forward. He exudes gin fumes from a three-martini lunch.

"Okay, get back to work."

Then it happens. If only I'd had breakfast, if only that boy reading *Dracula* had invited me to suck his cock, if only the boss at this instant did not look so much like a pig, perhaps *then* I wouldn't have had to eat him.

A CRUCIAL TURN

Here my tale takes a crucial turn. If I described the demise of James Flanigan, president of the Research Spectacle, in minute and clinical detail (e.g., His eyes bulge as my jaw distends twice and slides over his head and shoulders. He begins to kick and squirm as my teeth prod him down my esophagus toward a more useful destination than he has heretofore occupied. He sweats profusely. etc.), still you wouldn't know if a) this is just a delusion on my part or b) I really *am* a lizard. But consider these points: Everyone's autobiography is fantastic, the more so the more detail that's provided. And what is more fantastic than the history of life?

Ten thousand million years ago, for no apparent reason, the universe exploded out of an infinitely dense hot dot. As the gases cooled and condensed into galaxies, stars, and planets, the universe continued to expand.

Skipping for the moment such conundrums as black holes and what holds the universe together at all, let us look at our own planet, earth, which is possibly unique (no one's sure) in developing oxygen, rain, oceans, and tiny one-celled marine creatures which gradually grew in size and complexity. Some, like the six-foot scorpions, began to creep out onto land. Biologists and geologists call this the Devonian period. There's only one giant continent, Pangaea. Amphibians rule the world. As volcanos and the crunching of the continental plates push up great mountain ranges (the Andes and Appalachians), reptiles appear.

After a couple hundred million years more, we enter the Mesozoic Era (260,000,000 B.C.), commonly called the Age of Dinosaurs. The word dinosaur, coined by Sir Richard Owen in 1841, derives from two Greek roots, *deinos* and *saurus,* meaning terrible lizard. They dominate the earth for the next one hundred and seventy million years, but humans don't realize this until the late nineteenth century because Christianity forbids the study of fossils. Even Baron Leopold Cuvier, who found the giant Meuse lizard, was a creationist who believed these creatures were forms God had tried out and rejected.

In the United States, dinosaur study dates from October 5, 1787, three months after the ratification of the U.S. Constitution, when Dr. Caspar Wistar found a fossil in Camden, New Jersey. Dinosaur fossils were popular attractions after the Civil War, although some displays were canceled due to Christian pressure groups.

Is not this condensed history at least as fabulous as *Tarzan at the Earth's Core* by Edgar Rice Burroughs? or *West of Eden* by Harry Harrison? Burroughs called his lizard men the Horib, Harrison called his the Yilane. Both species were callous and unemotional. What can't be denied is that our planet's biological system developed for three thousand five hundred million years without human intelligence. Human civilization's puny four thousand-year history is hardly a strong argument for the evolutionary advantage of either intelligence or sensitivity—at least as humans define it.

But then I wonder and feel confused, hardly a saurian characteristic. Why were we, and a succession of other creatures, thrown up from the primordial soup? Are the slithering squeaks and cries one hears in *Saint of the Pit* by Diamanda Galas an archetypal memory of Mesozoic sound

16

bites, or a harbinger of sings to come? How one answers gives meaning, without which life would be unbearable.

When Gilgamesh parted the waters...

When Ptah spat out his name...

When the beginning was the Word and the Word was with God...

When it was a truth universally acknowledged that a single man in possession of a good fortune must be in want of a wife...

When you called me Ishmael...

When the red, red robin comes bob, bob bobbin' along...

Then either I'm a stranger in town or we've embarked on a pretty weird trip. And while I may not know who I am, I hope you'll agree that my narrative is a heroic struggle against the forces of entropy.

ADDITIONAL LIZARD HISTORY

The Cotylosaurus of the Triassic period (260-210,000,000 B.C.) is the ancestor to reptiles, dinosaurs, lizards, and birds. Actual lizards, as well as mammals, don't appear until the Jurassic period (about one hundred and fifty million years ago).

Reptiles, being cold blooded, constantly move about to attain their desired body temperature. Movement, however, burns energy and increased size retains heat. Thus (at least until the break-up of Pangaea into today's seven continents) it was an advantage to be big. Comets, not stupidity or bulimia, did in the dinosaurs.

Reptile evolution advanced because of the egg. The young were born ready to fight and get food. Lizards, however, were more varied in structure, form, and function. Basilisks, for instance, can run on their hind legs over land or water. Lizards also became more social than other reptiles. Female lizards

17

brood their eggs, which they are able to identify with the tip of their tongue.

Lizards and snakes are both great bluffers, masters of concealment and flight. Some change bodily shape to scare off enemies. The horned toad, for instance, puffs up grotesquely, and can squirt blood from its eyes to a distance of seven feet. Many lizards have detachable tails to confound enemies; others have spiny tails which they thrash about. Most lizards are agile and aggressive when hungry. Only the chameleon cautiously stalks its prey, striking at the last second with its popgun tongue.

Lizards announce sexual interest by means of color disparities. Bright crimson, the preferred color, may be displayed on a permanent (male spiny lizard), seasonal (female leopard lizard, male collared lizard), or momentary basis (iguanids and agamids).

When courting, male lizards slink close to the ground with their tails raised. They lick the passive female to arouse her, then grip her on the neck and groin so that mating can begin. The penises of snakes and lizards unfold from their tails like little fingers. Gecko lizards sing love songs.

Mythologically, in the West lizards symbolize a fearful, voracious chaos; in the East the power of samadhi. Maybe it's their deepest selves that Westerners fear—a fear they project onto their saurian neighbors? The human fetus goes through all earlier stages of evolution in the womb. Robert Bly argues that a reptile brain underlies, and is perhaps stronger than the more recently evolved human brain.

The largest present day lizard is the Komodo Dragon, which reaches a length of ten feet. Iguanas can grow to be three to four feet long and the Gila monster, the only poisonous lizard, may grow to a length of two feet. Most lizards are tiny, only a few inches in length.

Dale Russell speculated in 1981 that if dinosaurs had not been wiped out by the comets, today they would walk upright, be about four and a half feet tall, and have a highly advanced technological civilization.

A PERSONAL MEDITATION

The above summarizes everything I learned in high school about lizards. Was it my heavily-lidded eyes, my expressionless face, or my dry, scaly skin that led me to identify with them? For as long as I can remember I've always felt like an outcast. While other children romped and played, I preferred to hibernate in my basement, or to lie lazily in the sun next to the outdoor public swimming pool and gaze at the attractive bodies of my peers. Apparently I mastered the art of camouflage early, because I seemed invisible to those around me.

Except to my mother, that is. Every night, after my bath, she'd make me stand naked on top of the toilet seat while she slapped Noxema on the rash on my buttocks and behind my knees. "This is just *terrible*," she'd moan. "This is *awful*."

Allergy tests indicated that my skin disliked wool (but then what lizard would?), and medicated Denorex shampoo (intended to relieve dandruff, seborrhea, and psoriasis) never eliminated the scaliness of my scalp. But I didn't complain. I stood passively while my mother applied her salves and unguents. I'm not sure if my passivity was due to a deficiency or an excess of feeling. I knew I'd be free of these humans eventually. For now, maybe it was better if they didn't know my true nature.

Turtles and fireflies were my favorite pets, the former because of how slowly they moved (and how they could pull their bodies into a shell when threatened), the latter because I enjoyed catching them and crushing them against my fingers to make fluorescent rings. But it was turtles I liked best. I imagined I was one when I tucked myself between the covers of a book.

When I couldn't physically escape from the torment of my peers, I found I could scare them off by puffing myself up with big words. I'd never dare call anyone an ass, for instance, but I might suggest that someone should take their jawbone and slay a thousand Philistines. I found that when people can't understand what you say they leave you alone.

I'm not sure when the suspicion I might be a lizard became an obsession. Maybe it was when this girl at a party said "Why don't you slink up a wall or something?" I discovered drugs in tenth grade and soon began to hang out in dark bars. It was then I first heard the term "lounge lizard." I also found that I could fix certain boys with my basilisk stare, sidle over to them, nuzzle their necks, and feel our penises begin to uncurl like beckoning fingers. A wonderful feeling, this lizard lust, related to the fall of Sophia (wisdom) through what gnostics called the Pleroma whereupon Sophia bore the Demiurge. Perhaps this feeling also motivated the grand ritual sacrifices of Montezuma, who ate only those young men he preferred in bed. In any event, the feeling was almost enough to make my life unmanageable.

Which takes me back to the problem with which I began this chapter—what in hell was I doing to my boss toward whom I felt *no* sexual attraction whatsoever?

For a long while we just glared at each other. If this had been a heresy trial he might have probed my intention and seen that my hunger had me poised on the edge of carnivorous violence. Or perhaps he *did* perceive this, which is why he backed off, finally mumbling, "Okay, just get back to work." Maddy heaved a sigh of relief.

"You really should come to a meeting with Tom and I," she scolded. "We'd *all* have been up Shit Creek if you'd have…"

"*I* don't have a problem," I snapped back. "That pig Flanigan has the problem."

For once Helga was fortunate not to understand what we were talking about.

20

−3−
ART, SEX & ROCK N' ROLL

After work I head for the Lizard Club, which is two blocks away. Maddy is right, it *was* a close call. But I haven't hit bottom yet. A couple Jagermeisters will hopefully restore me to sanity. The cobalt mirror behind the bar makes everything look dark and foggy, like a Kirlian photograph or maybe a hologram. The mysterious stranger who's put three roses and a bottle of cognac on Edgar Allen Poe's grave every January nineteenth since 1949 would feel right at home here, especially since "Hoodoo Talk" is playing on the jukebox.

> Don't set me up
> Don't hold me down
> Don't tie me up
> Let me out
> Slash up anything
> Watch out
> Bend the bones
> Bend the structure
> Leather hand so good to feel
> Leather, you feel so real

All the bars in town, at least the ones I like, are fronts for heretical sects. The Lizard Club is Manichean. Club Chaos, Arian. Club Uranus is Apollinarian, and Screw—well, it's rumored to be the last holdout of the Borborites. DJs have to play music espousing their club's theology or they're exiled to Brisbane, where even the gecko's love song is frowned upon.

I no sooner down my first Jagermeister than in comes Jerome, wearing a cobra skin tube top with matching mini-skirt and hip length boots. She's as frail as a ghost and her long, stringy hair falls over her naked shoulders like a collection of the whips that anchorites used to flagellate themselves. The kohl around her eyes would heat Leningrad all winter.

"Ooo Baby, whadaya think," Jerome squeals, twirling around to show me her new outfit. I answer by paraphrasing a new song by Coil, a band especially popular with us Manicheans ever since Clive Barker rejected their "Hellraiser" soundtrack as "too scary."

"Your wandering mind is over the border, a mind like a cemetery where the corpses are turning."

"Oh doll," Jerome gushes, batting her three inch eyelashes. "You say the *sweetest* things." Then she elaborates on my doctrine using as her text a stanza from Wire:

> Something snaps over the horizon
> Something broke just out of reach
> like a dam on the boundary
> a rope on the border
> over and over just out of reach.

I could tell Jerome was still in high spirits from getting crowned Empress Tyrant, and from the critical success of her Art Lick show. Lizards all over town were still talking about the interview I did with her, which I must say puffed up my head, although hopefully not so much as William Tell's older, less fortunate son. In case you missed it, here's an excerpt:

JEROME'S INTERVIEW

ME: What are your favorite movies?

JEROME: I like everything—Fassbinder, Killer Clowns from Outer Space, Barbarella. There's a Marquis de Sade movie I can't remember the name of (Liz Taylor played de Sade—it was during her pulchritudinous period) and I love show tunes too, movies with the big dance numbers.

ME: A lot of elements in your work are appropriated. Do people ever steal your ideas?

JEROME: I hope so. My friend Adam Klein had a group named Anti-product that used found paintings and I stole a lot of ideas from them too. Oh, the relief of no longer being the sole master of one's text!

ME: You have a lot of Catholic iconography in your paintings. What's your family background?

JEROME: I have ten brothers. My mother goes to mass daily. I used to do missionary inner city work in Cleveland. I also used to teach sculpture classes to a group of retired nuns. But I think spirituality is very personal and that people should keep it to themselves more. It's become too much of a fashion lately.

ME: What do you mean? Isn't that a Quietist position?

JEROME: Oh pooh! You might as well say I'm a saurian reincarnation of Arius, since I'm tall and beautiful with a melancholy thoughtful face and a sweet, impressive voice. And arrogant as hell.

But seriously, how many Councils has Pope Lewis called on this Arian heresy anyway—five or six at least. First he anathematized and exiled Arius, then Athanasius, and all for want of a diphthong: Is Christ *homoousian* or *homoiusion*? Then along comes Aetius who says Christ is *anomois* (totally different from the Father and capable of sin) only to be answered by Basil who argues Christ is *homoean* or *like* the Father. Then the Pneumatomoachians claimed that the Holy Spirit isn't divine. Can you beat that? Well I'm getting pretty sick of it all myself. It used to be you were only ostracized if you made the wrong fashion statement; now you can't go anywhere without being theologically interrogated. Honey, I just wanna *dance*!

ME: Was the hair in your piece "That hair-do's out of control" real hair?

JEROME: You better believe it, girl. They did that all the time in the middle ages—ground up the bones and fingernails of saints and mixed them in with the paint. The souls of demons and angels are invoked and enclosed in the sacred images so that the idols may have the power to do good and evil. But my favorite is "Flossing with Jesus." I worked five years on that and it was no small coup when I got a piece of Christ's original dental floss which I of course verified by the carbon 14 method.

ME: What about the dark elements in your work—violence, dismemberment, and so on?

JEROME: Ah, my exit into the darkness of night; but which night? not that permanent night whose name may not be pronounced, a remote reference to nocturnal states for the saurian looking for the vague melancholy of the soul, profound, indiscernible darkness of being and love. In that case I should have made a theatrical exit, a false exit. I must put up with it, call on whatever signs may make it acceptable. Even so, it's an opening into some-thing. One can't deceive oneself with impunity for the imposition was there at the outset—make punishment the basis of one's only chance of salvation.

ME: Tell me about your campaign for Empress?

JEROME: Well, I think they were a little shocked when I handed in my application. But they were very nice, me being a Borborite and all. The receptionist said maybe I'd look nice in a little make-up and a nice dress. I thought, how about a *lot* of make-up and a *little* dress. When I showed up for my interview in a tube top and with my pubic hair showing they were really shocked. You'd think they'd never seen a lizard with pubic hair before.

I guess you're supposed to be a trend setter. One person asked what I'd think of seeing a lot of older, overweight men in tube tops. I said I thought it would be great. When I asked what they expected me to wear, they showed me a picture of Queen Elizabeth. How dowdy! I told them I had a full length see-through gown which looked really neat when I wore a bit of black lace and fishnet stockings underneath. Someone said maybe it would be okay if I wore a slip. I thought they said *whip*.

But I enjoyed the whole process. I think they're great—that whole thing. And they were very pleasant to me, I really have to give them credit for that.

ME: Do you find it difficult being a legend in your own time?

JEROME: Oh no, I think every lizard should. Like the life of people's brains—a different organization, a different balance, the amateur can only find his way around them with difficulty. Compare the brain to a souffle. You put it in the oven at around the Age of Reason. It rises very gently, swells, dilates until it gets to the age of adulthood, which varies with every individual, then it gradually sinks and ends up quite flat, or else burned, which was certainly the case with Marie and her master.

What's going to become of them? I was only speaking of it the other day to Lewis, who said that in serious cases where there's no family the mayor has to intervene but he'd never dare risk it after all the tales you hear about madmen barricading themselves into their houses. He could just see Monsieur Tom and his maid armed with shotguns and refusing them access to Club Uranus. Well it's times like these I'm glad I'm a Borborite and can suck cock without guilt.

* * * * *

I look at my watch and realize I'd better leave if I'm to make my Political Propaganda class at S.F. State tonight. It's 6:30 P.M. now, so 2nd street is almost deserted. Then, about a block from Montgomery Station, I realize I have to defecate.

I always seem to be either in a bathroom or feeling the need for one. My flatulence has been very persistent too, probably due to my irregular eating habits and my preference for raw fruits and vegetables (partly because I enjoy chewing and partly because these can be eaten without having to cook them). However, it crosses my mind that I should get myself checked for parasites. I may have picked them up from sex or from eating too many cockroaches.

But it's my incontinence that's most embarrassing. We lizards have a physical inability to control our sphincters as I was reminded recently when I reviewed the *Liquid Eyeliner* show. Let's just say this reviewer was quite uncomfortable, which had nothing to do with the art.

Fortunately I spot a dumpster up an alley. But after retiring behind it to do my business, I'm hungry again and there's no time to rummage about for food if I'm to make my class. It must be the legacy of Sophia's fall that forces us to occupy so much of our time trying to fulfill some physical need or other; which reminds me of another bit of shriek opera by Diamanda Galas:

26

The devil's an impotent man
He tries to make you uncertain
so that your hands shake.
And then he tells you you're insane.

Arius, who lived in the fourth century A.D., was the first to realize pop music's great potential in disseminating propaganda. Sailors sang his ditties as they travelled from port to port. Soon everyone was Arian. (No wonder conservatives want to control song lyrics.)

Unfortunately, like most pop stars, Arius came to a bad end. On the eve of his reinstatement as the Bishop of Alexandria, he suddenly fell ill and retired into a public privy. While his servant waited outside, Arius fell through the privy opening and into the sewer below. At least that's what his ideological opponent Athanasius said.

By now the M car's arrived and I'm lucky to find not only a seat but also a copy of today's paper. I immediately turn to Dear Abbey.

DEAR ABBEY: I just read "Losing Patience" who complained his 14-year-old daughter from another marriage was spending the summer with him so that he and his new wife had to put their love making on hold. You said he should get over his "hang-ups." I disagree.

My wife and I also require privacy because when we have sex she moans and screams. We have to send our kids to the movies when we do it. However, once a neighbor asked what was going on and I replied that the noise was caused by my son's gecko lizards. Do you think God will forgive my little white lie?—MOANERS IN COHASSET

27

DEAR MOANERS: Some boys breed trouble, some lizards, but unless your neighbor is retarded, I bet he already knows who the real moaners in Cohasset are. But even if you could fool all of your neighbors all of the time, you'd never fool God who punishes liars with everlasting hellfire.

Nothing like reading Dear Abbey to make me glad I'm a lizard!

Behind me three noisy teenagers argue over who has the best Addidas and who smells least like cat pee. To my right a student from State wearing a Matisse print shirt by Zylos (which comes in burnt orange, saffron yellow, apple green, and bleached oak) is telling his girlfriend (who is wearing an Escada drop-shoulder paisley sweater in multiple colors) that there's been a rash of bizarre accidents caused by people trying to stage stunts for *America's Funniest Home Videos*. And in the seat in front of me two old Russians, wearing a tattered tweed topcoat and a brown and green plaid hunting jacket respectively, discuss the day's races.

"I'd *never* bet on The Lessons of History," says the unshaven one. "That horse has *never* won a race. I told you to go with Toxic Waste but you wouldn't listen."

I wish I could squirt blood on them all through my horned toad eyes, or incinerate them all with my cyborg laser eyes, or simply disappear into my reflection in the window like Kenneth Anger escaping the nuclear apocalypse through his demon tunnel. Instead I wait for my stop at S.F. State, whereupon I disembark and go to my class in the Humanities Building only to discover a note on the door announcing that tonight's class is canceled, which means I've made this whole trip for nothing.

So I walk to the Student Union (one of the ugliest buildings ever to grace a college campus—it looks all crumbled, as if the *Challenger* crashed into it), and go downstairs two flights for something to eat. The only thing open is Wong's Oriental Delight, where a decidedly *undelighted* looking girl serves me a styrofoam plate of curried chicken over rice. This relieves my hunger but makes me feel queasy, maybe because of the fluorescent lighting overhead or the noise and blinking lights of the Nintendo games being played next to the dining area. Or maybe it's because as I eat I begin reading in H. G. Wells' *War of the Worlds* a description of Martian heat rays incinerating large sections of English countryside.

In any event, the food and sensory overload again make me feel an urgent need to answer nature's call ("Get thee hence to the land of Mount Moriah," as God commanded Abraham), so I trek back upstairs to the bathroom where I enter the next to the last stall, sit down, and begin reading the graffiti. Crude drawings of big penises, etc. The rest is mostly racist. Occasionally someone's combined genres giving hostile descriptions of alleged homosexual activities as practiced by or between various species and ethnic groups.

Then I hear it, faintly at first, the tapping of a foot in the next stall and a labored breathing. My saurian doors of perception immediately open. Now I smell the unmistakable exudation of sweat from a glans penis and the slightly saltier odor that emanates from mammalian armpits when sexual arousal occurs.

I waste no time in climbing up on the toilet seat to peer over the lime green metal wall separating us, and there below me I see the boy I saw reading *Dracula* on the bus this morning. His mouth hangs open, his eyes are rolled back. His face shines with an expression I've seen only twice before: once in a Borborite orgy, and once in a photo of a Chinese torture called "The ordeal of the Hundred Pieces," on page 204 of the City Lights edition of George Bataille's *The Tears of Eros*.

29

The boy is masturbating his cock, which is as stiff as a piece of bamboo. His testicles are as tight and round and shiny as a pair of leechee nuts.

Faster than Robin could exclaim, "Leapin' Lizards, Batman!" I'm over that stall and going down on that boy with more gusto than any lizard cyberpunk specifically designed and engineered for exactly this purpose.

–4–

OF DREAMS & BORBORITES

"This happened! This *really happened*!"

I was talking to Maddy the next morning at work. "It was awful (to quote my mother). I got so carried away with last night's boy that I gobbled up a whole forest, so to speak, including some indigenous ferns, several wall flowers, and a couple of capricious striplings who happened in by mistake. I could hardly waddle back to catch the M afterwards."

"I dunno," Maddy mused. "You're going to eat that whole campus if you're not careful. Sure you don't want to come to a meeting with Tom and me? I got in the program after I ate two mothers, three children, and a wino in a laundromat one night."

"I don't think I'm ready for that yet," I answered. I was sure I could handle this problem on my own, if I just stayed away from The Lizard Club and ate better breakfasts.

"You sure it wasn't just a dream?" Jim interjected. "I dreampt I was in a Heavy Metal band last night, and it was so real I couldn't hear anything when I woke up."

"I think I know the difference between dreams and reality," I snapped, and to prove my point I gave Jim a short lecture on dream theory.

A SHORT HISTORY OF DREAMS

The first dream treatise was a five volume work written by Artemidorus, who saw dreams as portholes into the future. He classified dreams about basilisks, birds, death, eating, feet, gold, hands, heads, mothers-in-law, olives, penises, reptiles, strangers, sex, and wheat. Sex dreams, he maintained, are about profit or power.

For instance, if you dream you fuck your wife and she's willing, that's good business. But if you dream you go to a brothel and can't leave, that's because brothels, like cemeteries, are places men have in common and where seeds perish. So it means death. Artemidorus also interpreted dreams of intercourse with animals, brothers (both younger and older), sons (top versus bottom), slaves, enemies and mothers.

Artemidorus believed that dreams were messages from the gods. Aristotle disagreed. If the gods really wanted to communicate with us, why wouldn't they be more careful in their choice of recipients? "A stitch in time saves nine," Artemidorus retorted; "Where there's a will there's a way." After a slew of such adages, Artemidorus concluded with a stretch of rhetoric so dazzling that it's been used ever since by academics and politicians as the most effective means to silence ideological opponents:

> I don't recall any—because I'm not changing my view,
> I'm just saying what's—what we may—you know,
> what's—everything's on the table. We may have to do
> something here. And—but if I were going to go back
> and say "Do it my way," we'd figure out a way that
> would be somewhat less controversial that this approach.
> But until that time, here I stand. So read my lips!

After this convincing rebuttal, Artemidorus's dream theory held sway for the next two thousand years. Then, in 1895, Sigmund Freud argued that dreams weren't about the future but about the past. All this stuff about birds, hands, and feet, said Freud, was merely displaced childhood fantasies. What everything's *really* about is *sex*. In our historically burdened times, Freud caught on like wildfire.

Carl Jung, Freud's colleague, raised the next obvious questions: If you're going to mine the past, why stop at childhood? Why not take on the whole collective unconscious and go back to Mesozoic times? A dream group in Los Angeles has done additional research on this and they claim that gay men dream differently than straight men. For instance, gay men see the anima as an ally, not an enemy. Some subjects also report favorable dreams about reptiles, lizards, and Bette Davis.

Most recently, psychological behaviorists and REM sleep experimenters (not to be confused with the pop group R.E.M. from Athens, Georgia) argue that dreams are just mental garbage. If dreams are about repressed fantasies, then why do almost all mammals show evidence of REM sleep? And why do newborn infants spend 50% of their sleep in REM whereas adults, who we might expect to be more sexually repressed, average only 15%? Finally, there's evidence that the cerebral cortex comes under the influence of the brain's lower centers during REM sleep, emitting random signals or bangs. So dreams may be merely a biological by-product, like a burp or hiccup.

In any event, dreams are credited with numerous scientific and artistic accomplishments: the invention of the sewing machine, Kekule's discovery of the molecular structure of benzene, Mozart's symphonies, and so on.

$\star$　$\star$　$\star$　$\star$　$\star$

"Those Borborites you hang out with," Maddy said when I'd finished. "Are you sure they don't aggravate your behavior?"

"Jerome, you mean?" I laughed nervously. "She's just an artist. Artists are *supposed* to be weird. But I don't really hang out with her, I just reviewed her show. I have to meet all kinds of weirdos when I write reviews for *SF Weekly* and other rags. But I don't take any of their heresies *seriously*."

(I was lying, of course. History has taught that heretics who don't lie—the Albigensians, etc.—soon perish.)

"Well tell me about these Borborites," Maddy pressed. "What do they believe?"

Not one to bypass any opportunity to display my photographic memory (much enhanced by all the memories I'd absorbed through imbibing the vital body fluids of countless young men over the years), I agreed. If I didn't, I feared that Maddy might decide to alleviate our boredom in coding B of A User Response Questionnaires by reciting once again the fate of all the original members of the first Soviet Central Committee after Stalin came to power in the 1930s.

A SHORT HISTORY OF THE BORBORITES (FROM A.D.100 TO THE PRESENT)

The Borborites (not to be confused with the later Bogomiles) were offshoots of the earlier gnostic Nicolaitan sect described as "hated by God" in the canonical *Book of Revelation*.[1] Several sources from the second and third centuries A.D. speak of the Nicolaitans' luxurious and dissolute living and their dualistic cosmology. The actual spinning off (according to the gnostic texts *Pistis Sophia* and *The Second Book of Jeu*) was marked

---

[1] Theodoret claims the Borborites derive from the Valentinian gnostics but gives no convincing proof of this.

by the consumption of semen and menstrual fluids as a holy sacrament.[2] Epiphanius says that one group of Nicolaitans proclaimed the general imperative of gathering "the scattered seed of Prunikos from bodies," or sexual excretions.

The theological advocacy and actual practice of sexual and dietary encraticism is well attested to in the second century and, despite Clement and Origen's more balanced attitude, often resulted in a demonization of sexuality. In short, if the body and physical world is hopelessly evil, as most Gnostics believed, then it made little difference what one did.

The Borborites rejected encratic orthodoxy as ineffective but were equally dissatisfied with the free play of sexual appetites as an expression of nihilism. They stressed the encratic emphasis on sexuality but claimed to be able to master it through careful, ritual exercise.[3] Finally, they believed that the spiritual power in the universe was most concentrated in semen.

But the key evidence concerning Borborite praxis comes from Epiphanius's first-hand description of their Alexandrian community in his *Panarion* (A.D. 370). Epiphanius describes the sect as widespread and well organized. Its adherents went under several names (the elite being the exclusively homosexual Levitai). Epiphanius's vivid description is so detailed it can hardly be dismissed as a prurient invention:

> At the moment of Consecration, the priest whipped out his member (referred to in the liturgy as The Pneumatic Drill). I had never seen anything so large. After the priest and church elders ejaculated into the chalice, all the congregation's males did the same with little cups

---

[2] *The Second Book of Jeu* further claims their true god is the "Third power of the Great Archon," the lion and pig-headed Taricheas.

[3] See possible connections with Carpocratians as well as tantric Buddhist practices in India during this period.

35

they brought with them. Everyone then drank deeply. Any residue left on a member's member was dutifully sucked off by boys who went round the congregation for that purpose. In some cases (for instance, if a boy's jaw got tired), it was deemed permissible to give him a good fucking. But the acolytes were generally quite zealous in the performance of their office. One could only wish orthodox congregations demonstrated such enthusiasm.

Epiphanius then quotes samples of Borborite biblical exegesis and cites their most revered texts, such as *The Dance of the Virgin Mary*, *The Gospel of Philip* (used by Borborite Levites as a formula for ascending the archonic spheres), *The Gospel of Eve* (linked to the Nag Hammadi *Thunder* tract; see Appendix A, at the end of this chapter), and so on.

As a result of Epiphanius's denunciation, the Borborites were expelled from Egypt. Theodoret claims that the orthodox were envious and feared they could not compete with the Borborites in attracting followers.

Shortly thereafter, in Syria, the Arian Aetius was soundly defeated in a debate with a Borborite Levite. His despondency was only lifted by his subsequent rhetorical victory over a Manichean notable. Saint Jerome and Bishop Theodore of Mopsuestia also refer to Borborites in Asia Minor. Theodore identifies them as followers of the crypto-Christian Simon Magus.

Wherever the Borborites appeared, they engendered energetic inquisitorial action. Mesrop, inventor of the Armenian alphabet, imprisoned and tortured them. If they remained recalcitrant they were branded, smeared in pitch, painted various colors (a punishment for their sacramentally rubbing themselves with semen), and exiled. Nestorius, in Constantinople, was distressed that "Borborites went freely into the Churches with the Christians," some even posing as clergy. As late as the twelfth century, Michael the Syrian, in his *Monophysite Chronicle*, says Borborites disguised as monks practiced unspeakable acts of promiscuity, magic, and ritual child murder. But most commentators could not bring themselves to describe their practices in detail. As Maruta of Mayperkat writes: "Because of their obscenity and defilement, great lasciviousness, abominable deeds, and foul works, and (because) they pour out the blood of babes for sorcery, I am excused from writing anything about them."

Only in Persia did the Borborites receive a temporary haven. They were said to have inspired the Sufi poet Rumi as well as *The Rubaiyat of Omar Khayyam*. They did not win favor with Mohammed, however, who allegedly warned one Borborite Levite to "get your cock out of my face."

For the next seven hundred and fifty years almost nothing was heard of the Borborites. Some believe their sect died out, but it's more probable that they went underground. Savonarola accused Pope Alexander IV of Borborite sympathies, and the later Swedenborgians, with whom William Blake was affiliated, share elements of Borborian cosmology. But we cannot assume every libertine eruption is due to a direct Borborite influence. Even in Walt Whitman's poetry, where the sacramental efficacy of semen seems clearly argued (cf. "The 29 bathers"), it is possible that other influences were at work.

In our own time, Borborite doctrines seem to have resurfaced with the hippie and gay liberation movements. In 1984, an anonymous tract was published in San Francisco under the title *Suck Mine & Live Forever* (see Appendix B, at the end of this chapter). This tract included a "Hippie Histomap," suggestions on how to establish secret Borborite societies, and so on. Finally, in 1989, Club Uranus and then

Screw opened—heretical offshoots of the Arian Club Chaos. Uranus encourages lascivious dancing and smearing the body with sperm-like substances; Screw shows films of Borborite rites. These institutions not only propagate Borborite doctrines in their music and rituals (e.g., that the world was created by angels, that semen is a spiritual sacrament, that one can dance one's ass into heaven, etc.), but actively recruit youth to the Borborite cause.[4]

Just as the Borborites of old were persecuted, the Borborites of today are anathematized by conservative politicians, by Christians, and even by orthodox elements within the gay community.[5]

★ ★ ★ ★ ★

---

[4] Although today's clubs retain a traditional separation of heterodox beliefs in their choice of decor and music, a new ecumenical spirit between them must also be noted. For instance, Club Chaos plays the song "I Gotta Big Dick" which may be interpreted as a mocking reference to the hypostatic union *or* as an invitation to Borborite excess. Habitues of these clubs also overlap.

[5] The following letter (*San Francisco Sentinel*, 7/28/90) documents the latter: "As a gay man I watched with Gay Pride as Sunday's Parade started but my pride turned to shame and embarrassment as the "Chaos" float came into view.... Although outrageous, erotic or suggestive displays are acceptable—lewdness has no place. The sight of men on a float playing with organs of which they appeared to be overly proud was offensive. It's high time the parade organizers laid down a code of conduct for this event to prevent such appalling displays of bad taste (which) also reinforces the worst public stereotype of the gay male: as a person whose brain is controlled by his dick."—R. Readman, SF.

APPENDIX A

Thunder, Perfect Intellect is a bizarre poem of two hundred verses which combines the rhetorical mode of omnipredication with a logic of antithetical paradox that negates the possibility of taking predication seriously. The poem begins:

> It is from the power that I, even I, have been sent
> And unto those who think on me that I have come;
> And I was found in those who seek me.
>
> . . . . .
> For it is I who am the first: and the last.
> It is I who am the revered: and the despised.
> It is I who am the harlot: and the holy.
>
> . . . . .
> For it is I who am acquaintance: and lack thereof.
> I who am reticence: and frankness.
> I am shameless: I am ashamed.

As these lines show, the text is a monologue concerned not with plot but with the building up of a contradictory persona. Modern interpretation stresses the combination of *ego eimi* and paradox as the text's salient feature, but half of the verses are a gnostic diatribe wherein the speaker disparages the reader's actions and attitudes. Finally, the fragmentary mythic framework at the beginning of the poem, as well as at the middle ("It is I who cry out: /And upon the face of the earth am being cast out"), and at the end ("For many and sweet are the passions which people restrain /Until they flee up to their place of rest/ And find me there/ And live, and not die again.") summarizes the soul's descent into the body and its reincarnational entrapment.

As Bentley Layton says of the narrator built up by this curious intersection of rhetorical modes:

First, she likes to talk! We may call her "she," but gender

is ultimately irrelevant since she is only a traveling voice. She is the savior of mankind; she saves by preaching, demanding a reorientation of mind and heart. She invites comparison with Isis and thence Dame Wisdom. She is an element within those to whom she is sent ... so that self-knowledge and knowledge of the savior may at least partly be the same ... [This] raises the acute question of whether or not one should take the text seriously. Or [does the text imply] the rejection of all value systems that are at home in the world?

Layton goes on to note that riddling was an important game in ancient Greek culture and cites some typical examples:

No one seeing sees me, but one who does not see beholds me.
One who does not speak speaks; one who does not run runs.
I am a liar, yet say all things true.
Solution—a dream.

In a lengthy exegesis, Layton argues that the *Thunder* text is a variant of the Eve riddles postulated in *The Gospel of Eve*. Both the speaker's puzzling genealogy and moral ambiguity reflect the widespread belief that the biblical Eve had disported with the devil, a belief which in gnosticism finds systematic expression in tandem pairs of female emanations called *pronoia: epinoia* (forethought: afterthought), or high and low wisdom. Epiphanius associates these contradictory personae with the Borborites' central dogma that one can attain the highest spiritual wisdom only by going into the gutters to suck cock.

* * * * *

APPENDIX B
(Excerpts from *Suck Mine* & *Live Forever*)

1) PLAN FOR THE DESTRUCTION OF ART:

> Create a 'zine called *New Hippies*.
> Oxymoron title reflects historical gyre.
> Raid symbolism outta the mouths of babes.
> Probe youth trying to recapture its youth.

Conduct interviews interspersed with porn and descriptions of moonscape. He was very shy at first and I was surprised he'd been a Student Government Rep. He wore t-shirts with incomprehensible poems magik-markered on them. I suggested he tatoo these directly on his body.

> Mauve sky main obstacle.
> May a moody baby doom a yam?
> Avoid buzzwords & fashion statements
> strobed with color as only content.

But interviews, unfortunately, are banal and trite. When he asked someone what it was like growing up in the 60s, they replied "We didn't." We last saw her on Halloween dressed as an American flag.

> Make a histomap of hippie happenings,
> holograms of impossible desires.
> When I read a 'zine called *Violent Silence*
> I fell in love with a boy with a body of gold.

Abandon interviews for overheard conversations. Change costumes, name, and hair color every day. Charles changes his name to Chameleon when he graffitis poems on city

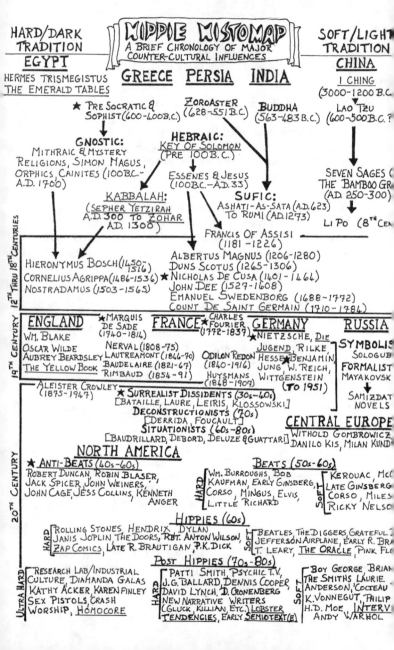

walls at night. I thought Creature was from the Black Lagoon but Gerbil says his girlfriend just called him that cuz he reminded her of a fuzzy little woodland creature.

> Marauding skateboarders mutilate language.
> Android bodyguards dance dangerously
> with zombies. Artistic mood fix
> no longer justifies self-mastication by
> atavistic vanguard.

Dress in dark clothes. Haunt cafes, art openings and poetry readings. Skirt current issues with clever repartee. Only tell the truth when you're too stoned to talk.

> Abandon a 'zine called *New Hippies.*
> Oxymoron title reflects historical grave.
> Reify destruction of logocentrism.
> Promote uncouth attempts to recapture ecstacy.

2) PLAN FOR URBAN GUERRILLA WARFARE:

1. Form secret society. Write principles of incorporation by randomly selecting phrases from *The Gospel of Eve.* Make of these what you can.

2. The main purpose of the society shall be to advance spiritually by the ingestion of sperm. This shall be the society's principal liturgical ritual.

3. The society's secondary purpose will be to demonstrate its indifference to the material world by celebrating uselessness in elaborate and carefully contrived charades. Suggested projects:

a) Portray favorite saint. In this guise, describe exquisite details of martyrdom.

b) Demonstrate how angels created the world by inventing novel rituals for love making, funeral and excretory rites, etc.

c) Develop new, surreptitious political actions. Put up posters that have no overt meaning save to expose the total moral bankruptcy and cynical manipulation of advertising.

d) Forge letters, fliers, and documents of rival political and theological sects so as to sow as much confusion as possible.

e) Kidnap respected orthodox leaders and photograph them in compromising sexual positions so as to discredit them.

4. Members must attend all meetings naked except for black masks. Never look at each other's faces and go only by the name given you by the society. Violation of this rule is grounds for expulsion.

5. Members shall be linked as lovers. These linkages may be celibate or not, duo or trio as members choose. Any member not in a linkage for over one month—but not subject to expulsion for violating society rules—shall become the "Pneumatic Drill" or leader for one month and entitled to autocratic control of all other members during this period. At the end of this time, the leader must submit to the desires of all other members and then be inducted into a linkage.

6. With the exception of the above rule, the society shall have no leaders. Society policy shall be decided democratically by secret ballot.

7. When society membership reaches seven, the society shall divide into two separate groups of three and four members respectively.

8. New members are to be inducted on basis of physical and spiritual beauty. Upon sponsorship by a current member, a prospective member must:

   a) Write a brief essay on their favorite debauchery.

   b) Create a performance celebrating their favorite angel in which they give themselves sexually to all society members.

   c) Betray someone close to them outside of the society.

9. Creative, arbitrary betrayals shall be considered an important part of the society's work.

10. All rules except rule 2 are subject to amendment by a unanimous vote of the members.

3) PLAN FOR THE DESTRUCTION OF SCIENCE:

For the past forty years, the leading sciences and technologies have been language centered: phonology and linguistic theories, cybernetics, algebra and informatics, computers and their languages, data banks, telematics, paradoxology, etc. Previous epistemological models [i.e., knowledge for human liberation (French philosophes); knowledge for the sake of knowledge (German Hegelians)] are now outmoded. Today knowledge is produced only to be sold, consumed only to be valorized in new production. In both cases, *the goal is exchange* (Lyotard). Marxism and capitalism

45

alike are enslaved to what Horkheimer calls "the paranoia of reason," Debord terms "the society of the spectacle," and Baudrillard demonstrates is the increasing unreality of image manipulation.

What needs to be advanced is a new Science of Play, of perpetual displacement, the end result of which will be a private Science of Erotics. This new science will be a negative doubling of the "exchange" or professional model. In short it will be a science of sabotage, irrationality and waste (Bataille).

A lover drifts but never forgets. Pursue etymological investigations with the obsessive passion of a poet. Clan destiny = clandestinity; transgression = / = stupidity. "Language is a system of symbols based on forgetting." (Theodore Thass-Theinemann)

* * * * *

When I finished recounting this history I was exhausted, although I communicated the footnotes, diagrams, and appendixes to Maddy by means of saurian telepathy so as to speed things up and not bore Jim. But at least my discourse enlivened an otherwise tedious day.

5:30 P.M.! I hit the street, my eyes ablur and aching from reading some three thousand five hundred questionnaires and writing "y," "1," "2," etc. all week. (Lizards have weaker eyes than humans, relying more on the sense of smell, so it's obvious I haven't chosen the most felicitous occupation.)

I feel tired.

I'm hungry.

I'm grouchy.

I can think of only three things: 1) Thank God it's Friday; 2) I must stay away from The Lizard Club at all costs; and 3) What in hell will I do instead?

–5–

WHO *IS* THAT LIZARD ANYWAY?

Whenever I talk too much I get angry. I get angry because words fail me. Whatever it is I want to say I don't know, but I talk and talk and it gets worse and worse, as if I were making a noose and putting my head in it but I can't stop. Maybe I talk so much because I feel lonely (even though lizards supposedly don't feel—another lie perpetuated by humans)? But how can I *not* feel lonely, when I eat everyone I'm attracted to? Even those I'm not attracted to. I decide that the first thing I should do is go home and take a shower, since I haven't done so in a week.

I get on the Muni and choose a seat behind the operator because the operator has a curtain which keeps him from seeing directly behind him. Sort of like blinders on a horse, and for the same reason, to avoid distraction. The reason I pick this seat is so the operator won't see me put my feet up on the seat and tell me to put them down.

When I get home I climb the three flights of stairs to my apartment, go into the bathroom, peel off my clothes, get into the shower and turn on the water. I'm glad it's hot, which isn't always the case. But something is wrong with the nozzle so that instead of the water coming out in a nice misty spray it shoots down in intense jet streams like sharp little knives. I don't know what to do about this. I yell out to A. to see if she knows, but get no answer, so I gather she's not home. Finally it gets so bad I plug the drain and turn the knob so that the water comes out of the faucet instead of the nozzle, but then I notice that the water is a scummy brown so I pull the plug and let it drain out.

I lie for a long time in the empty tub, not feeling motivated to move, thinking about nothing, savoring the unique ambience that hot steam brings out in mould, talcum powder, pee around the toilet base, toothpaste, Peridex Oral Rinse, Gillette lemon-lime shaving cream, Lysol disinfectant, and A's Joboba Swiss Formula hair conditioner. I start to doze; not going completely under, but under enough so that when I come to I'm struggling to recall what it was I was thinking cuz I'm sure it would make a great story if I could just get it down, but by this time it's already slipping away so that now that I have this pen and paper it's nothing but a few jumbled words. And I'm tormented that I can't get my subconscious to work like this when I'm awake.

Finally I get up and dry off, wondering if it's still early enough to do anything. I dig through my Hefty bag filled with clean clothes and pull out a yellow shirt, a pair of pants, and two socks that don't have holes. My selection is fairly limited since I haven't done laundry for awhile. I put these on.

Then I go into the kitchen to the fridge and take out one of those pots I like to keep going for weeks, eating some and adding more, until finally I begin to worry that some fungi or harmful bacteria may have started to grow. Tonight I decide to finish it off. This batch contains some vegetables and greasy chicken from the Lebanese grocery down the street. I put it on the stove, then rumage in the sink for a plate and spoon. All my dishes are dirty and it's hard to wash them because the sponges are also dirty. I've used them so often to remove grease from the stove that now everything, dishes and sponges alike, is caked with grease. Then, too, several sponges have been chewed by mice, probably for the grease. Finally I get a bowl clean enough to eat out of and I fill it with stew, only now realizing I could have saved time and energy by eating out of the pot. Afterwards I feel queasy again and have to go to the bathroom.

On my way, I notice a letter sitting on the kitchen table. Since it's postmarked Burma and addressed to me, I assume it's from my ex. It's written on that blue tissue-thin paper that doubles as an envelope, so I have to be very careful tearing it open. I take it into the bathroom to read while I sit on the can.

Dear Steve,

As I sit here in Rangoon, attired in an orange saffron robe in the dilapitory shade of a banyan tree, I can hear mosquitos, birds and merchants haggling in a distant market. Be not lazy, I tell myself. Can honesty ever be attained? Don't know. Ever & ever are these 26 letters a rope unable to form the lasso of language.

From my window at night I can see the moon. Gazing at it, I think of you. How are things in lizard land—still hopping I hope?

If you haven't noticed, each sentence of this letter begins with letters of the alphabet in sequence. *Joie de vivre*, to construct one's life as carefully as a poem. Kinkiness is all I ever wanted from you & you sure gave it. Little did we know destiny would tear us apart. Mainly I just want to say I hope this didn't hurt you too much. Nothing was further from my intentions. Only, as Gertie Stein said (hee, hee), "It takes a lot of work being a genius—you gotta sit around so much doing nothing."

Pain in my legs ceased after my 3rd day of sitting zazen. Quit fighting it, I told myself. Reality will get more rubbery once you get the hang of it.

"Sweeping" is another form of meditation some monks here favor. The deal is to place your hand everywhere over your body starting at the top of your head and working down feeling everything under your hand intensely, then letting go. Until mind & body drop away, you'll not taste the truth of the Tathagata's words. Very saurian, huh?

Wheezing from cigarettes.

Xenomorphic with desires.

You know a completely banal & unexpected thought just hit me. Zookeepers are extremely rare here in Rangoon.

yours,
Squirmy

ps—As for that Swami I told you about, he returned to India where he was detained by tax inspectors in the southern city of Madras on suspicion of violating the country's foreign women.

Damn that twit! Shoulda known better than to trust anyone named Squirmy. Turning the letter over, I pen a quick response in case he ever gives me his return address:

Darling, I had grapefruit juice for breakfast.
Darling, darling, it had high fructose corn syrup, citric acid, pectin, ascorbic acid, canthaxanthin, sodium, & traces of Vitamin A, Thiamine, Riboflavin, niacin & calcium in it.
Darling, do you notice every sentence of this letter begins with "D"?
Damn shame I didn't eat you when I had the chance!

By now it's getting late, so if I want to do anything I better hurry. I put on my shoes and dark topcoat with the torn lining, shove a book into my pocket, and head into the hall past the cats and downstairs out the door.

By the time I get to the corner, three winos have spare changed me. Now some Mexican kid is asking for a cigarette, but I can smell it's not really a cigarette he wants. So even though I don't smoke anymore I chat with him awhile till finally he affirms that kids today mumble their speech with their lips and teeth running words together without pause or distinction in such a way that a foreigner, though he understood English tolerably well, would be obliged to have recourse to a third party to explain what the speaker had said in his own tongue. I don't know why I've gotten into this stupid conversation. I just wanted to go to Cafe Macando for a cup of coffee.

I finally break away—"Gotta do a drug deal," I say and, "No you can't come"—and when I get to the cafe I'm relieved to find it's not as late as I thought. Only ten P.M. I get a cafe latte and sit down at a table by the window. Then it happens. Maybe it's my tinted glasses, my dead face, or my thinning hair when I comb it straight back. Or maybe it's the fact that I sometimes rub my forehead like a bomb when I read. Whatever, some kid inevitably walks over and asks if I'm Hunter S. Thompson.

"I'm imitating the past," I say. "I'm a 50s zombie from outer space. I used to be weird but now I just wanna be hip and normal like everyone else. My real name is Count Zero."

"Are you okay?" the kid asks, backing off.

"Sit down," I say, grabbing his skinny arm. "Let me tell you how it started. May, 1956, the year of 'Heartbreak Hotel,' 'Hound Dog,' 'Be-bop-a-lula': an obscure ex-trucker calling himself Nervous Norvus cuts 'Transfusion' for Dot. Within two weeks it sells half a million and Nervous (aka Jimmy Drake) is featured in *Life*. Then he vanishes from rock history.

"Nervous wasn't the first to sing about fast cars, but he was the first to use hideous sound effects—screeching tires, smashing metal, etc.—and his chorus, '*Transfusion, transfusion/ I'm just a solid mess of painful contusions*,' had hip postscripts like: '*Shoot me the juice, Bruce... Slip me the blood, Bud... Put a gallon in me, Allen.*' California's governor gave him a plaque for promoting highway safety but we kids knew better. Nervous sang terrific songs (his last, `Fang,' was later the name of a punk band), but when *Life* asked how he got his ideas he said, 'Sitting in the backyard going ump, ump.'

"See what I mean? Nervous failed to establish an oppositional language praxis in regard to the interview. Elvis, by contrast, became famous for biting a reporter's hand. At the same time, all Punk—the dark side of Rock, the irony of New Wave, the crashing of Industrial—derives from Nervous Norvus. That this plump-faced Buddy Holly without glasses disappeared without a trace is to his credit. He knew negativity would be big someday and he didn't want pimply teenagers camping on his doorstep offering him their bodies like they later did Kerouac."

I pause for breath, seeing from the kid's sweaty eyes that I've made a mistake. He just wanted my autograph and to chat brainlessly about drugs and target practice. Why'd I have to get so preachy? Twenty-year-olds hate to hear about anyone before David Bowie, so I decide to take a different tack.

"You come here often?"

"Some."

"Whadya think about lizards?"

Another silence.

"Ya know I'm pretty good with an Uzi and William Burroughs is terrific with his Borneo blow gun but for sheer speed and accuracy, nothing beats the chameleon's tongue. A chameleon your size could pick off a fly blindfolded at forty feet."

The kid's eyes light up. I knew this would grab his attention. But what I really want to talk about is Blue Movie, who I saw at the Firehouse last week. I was surprised how sharp their sound's become. Rich Ferguson, their poet/drummer, used to go nuts on stage, a real maniac. Now he's controlled berserk, half naked and painted up like a Borborite. I stood in the corner with my dark glasses and long dark topcoat while sixteen-year-old girls whipped me with their whirling dervish hair. Here, on the cafe stereo, an El Salvadoran folksong is followed by some group I never heard of singing Gregorian chant to lame lounge music. It's intended to make you feel slightly nauseous—like a David Salle painting.

"What are you reading?" The kid still thinks I'm Hunter S. Thompson and doesn't wanna leave yet, even though I *am* acting a bit adverb deleted.

"*Literal Madness* by Kathy Acker. We used to play chess up the street."

Actually, I was glad to stop reading cuz Kathy's porn makes me nervous. You get that way when you can't decide if you're a lizard or not, or when you realize getting laid is just another cranked up remnant of nostalgic romanticism. It's like Alfred E. Newman said once, "Show me a trunk murderer and I'll show you a sloppy packer."

"Do you know Patti Smith?"

"Can I be perfectly honest for a minute?" The kids's eyes widen as I lean forward over the table. Maybe he smells my B.O., which not even a shower of rusty brown sewage was able to alleviate.

"Y-ya, sure."

"I had this weird dream last night." I stare intently into the kid's eyes. "I'm in Columbia with this babe named Camille who goes into the jungle to pick flowers. I really was there once and this Camille had long blond hair, wore long white dresses, and went into the jungle every day to pick flowers. I'm serious.

"Well, in my dream Camille tells me there's a tribe of people I should meet so I follow her into the jungle to find them. They're very happy cuz they don't know anything about the outside world. No TV, no magazines, no Xerox machines, no blockbuster special effects movies starring Arnold Schwarzenegger or milk cartons with the faces of missing

53

children printed on them. It's paradise! They think I'm a spirit from another world which in a way, of course, I am.

"Anyway, this tribe is ruled by twins: one blond, cute and charming; the other dark, ugly and grouchy. The dark twin glowers at us but the blond hugs us warmly and shows us around the village. Camille and I can't help but fall in love with him and he seems pretty hot for us too. But being civilized as we are, we flip a coin as to who will go with him first. Camille wins so I go back to our hut to wait my turn.

"Then the dark twin comes in and says 'Watch out. My brother, he funny. He always mean the opposite of what he say.'

"'Whadaya mean?' I figure he's just jealous.

"'You no believe? Look through yon window of my brother's hut.'

"So I go look and see Camille and the blond twin getting it on. Very hot. I mean he's got a dick the size of a Tyrannosaurus's arm. He could lift four hundred pounds with it, easy. But suddenly blondie's arms and legs turn spidery and, well, it's a pretty gruesome sight. So I split but feel very sad, not only cuz I'll miss Camille, but because blondie seemed really sincere, not just putting on a front like most guys ya meet. So whadaya think my dream means?"

"Well, ah... " The kid swallows. "Maybe you should stop taking drugs for awhile."

"I stopped three years ago."

"Well," the kid swallows again. "It's a weird dream alright. Anyway, it's been great meeting you, Mr. Thompson, cuz I've always been a big fan."

"Ya, thanks. Anytime."

I'd have liked to end this chance encounter on a happier note but, while I'd heroically managed to keep my tail between my legs, I'd opened my big mouth again and, as usual, my big mouth betrayed me.

-6-

A DELICIOUS DIGRESSION

I lied.

I told the kid I was alive when Nervous Norvus sang "Transfusion." Actually I wasn't born until November 22, 1963, the day Jack Kennedy got splattered all over Jackie's strawberry pink suit and matching pillbox hat causing her such consternation that she scrambled onto the trunk of the Lincoln Continental, accidentally kicking the remains of her husband's head in the process. She later told the Warren Commission that she was just trying to retrieve a bit of Jack's brain. But that too was a lie. In her moment of truth, Jackie proved as desperate as the rest of us even though later, at the hospital, she got an iron grip on herself and refused to change out of her bloodstained outfit saying, "I want the world to see what they did to my husband."

That's how I feel all the time.

Only for me, instead of going shopping at Bloomingdales, a Mesozoic wind stirs in my veins and I feel, against all my best intentions, pulled towards—The Lizard Club. That's *my* black hole sucking me in under its event horizon.

I enter the lush darkness and head for the bar. In the cobalt mirror I can vaguely see Jerome, Diet, Bad, Donna Tello, and lizards I've never met and know only by smell, gathered around me. When things get really crazy this is one place a lizard can unwind. A new song by The Pelagians blares from the jukebox:

Sandra Bernhard has big feet
stomping to Madonna's beat.
Karen Finley freaks us out
where she puts that sauerkraut.

Money, sex, Born Again,
Works our nerves Pelagian.
God gives lizards just one chance
So get the Word and dance, dance, dance.

How will the Bishop of Hippo top this? His last single, "Lord help me, but not yet" didn't do too well, though I've heard it's been played at Uranus.

I order a gin and tonic. As I fish in my pocket for change, I'm accosted by Anonymous and Synonymous Jones, the Club's Performance Art twins.

"Oh Steve," moans Anonymous. "Give us some new ideas for our act. The boss wants more 'umph.'"

"How 'bout doing something on the secrets of San Francisco," I reply. "Or maybe on the secrets of syntax."

"*Sin* tax?" Synonymous squeals. "I thought President Bush promised 'No new taxes.'"

"That was last week."

"How 'bout doing something on Steve's ex, Squirmy." The new voice belongs to Donna Tello, a three hundred pound komodo dragon who's just joined us.

"Now *there's* an idea," I agree. "If Squirmy was president, you'd have Pee Wee Herman as his chief-of-staff and Mr. Magoo as his appointments secretary. Suzanne Vega would be his Secretary of Defence and..."

"Don't forget Martha Raye," Anonymous interjects. "She could be his Surgeon General. (In case you haven't heard, she's suing David Letterman for suggesting that she doesn't use condoms.)"

"It would take more than a condom to cover Martha's mouth," Synonymous sighs. "It would take a tent!"

"She's just kicking up a fuss so she'll get some fan mail,"

Anonymous continues. "It's like that *Burns & Allen* episode on TV last night. George feels bad cuz he hasn't gotten any fan mail so Gracie gets Blanche to write a fan letter. But Blanche's husband, Harry, finds it and gets jealous, though not as jealous as Violet MacGonegal's husband, who comes after George with a gun. So Violet rushes over to warn Gracie, saying 'Your husband said some very intimate things to me on the phone,' to which Gracie replies 'Don't worry. He does the same thing with me.'"

"Was that the show where Gracie calls Detective Sawyer at one A.M. because she's lost her bobby pin and the detective says she should have her head examined?" Donna asks.

"That's the one," Anonymous says. "And Gracie does, and she finds it. Now where was I?"

"Oh *girl!*" Synonymous cries, grabbing her twin by the arm. "We're on in five minutes!"

"What are those two like in bed," Donna asks me as they scurry off.

"They like bodies by Fisher and brains by Mattel. That way their tricks are too dumb to rat on them."

"*Eddie* Fisher?" Donna's eyebrows arch two octaves.

"No, he's the one who dumped Debbie for Liz—Liz Taylor I mean. But she ate him alive and then ran off with Mike Todd."

The lights dim and the jukebox is unplugged. Unlike Uranus, where the Go-Go boys dance in raised cages, Lizard Club dancers do their thing in a five by seven foot pit at the far end of the bar. If anyone gets bored, they urinate on the performers. A green spot illumines the smelly pit as Jerome announces the act:

"I'm proud to introduce Anonymous and Synonymous Jones who will tonight dramatize a poem by Eliza Pittsinger, a feminist who lived in San Francisco in the 1860s. The poem, *Kissing the Pope's Toe,* got Pope Pius XI to cancel his visit to our fair city. Hopefully, tonight's show will as effectively hex our theological opponents."

Anonymous steps into the pit carrying a gold staff. She's dressed in a white robe and little white skull cap and leads Synonymous, who wears a spiked collar and a G-string, on a leash. Jerome reads the poem as the twins pantomime it.

> A wonderful toe doth the Pope possess!
> Kiss it ye vassals and then confess!
> Unbosom your secrets to bigots and knaves.
> 'Tis a custom they cherish of making you slaves.

As Jerome reads, "Pope," Anonymous parts her robe revealing a huge erection kept hard by a rhinestone studded cock ring. But marvelous as this is, my attention wanders to the opposite side of the pit. There, in the shadows, I see a kid in a pony tail who's a dead ringer for Squirmy. A bit taller maybe. I make my way across the bar until I'm next to him.

"Been here before?" I ask nonchalantly.

"What an 80s question," the kid replies scornfully. "It's like 'What kinda work d'ya do?'"

"So what's a 90s question?"

"In the 90s we're too cynical to ask questions."

The kid's eyes are hard and hungry. He has a big nose and fleshy, sullen lips. The bluish glow of my gin and tonic matches the glow of his white tee-shirt which is emblazoned with a photo of the band Wire. Under the black light the photo sinks into his skinny chest like a gaping hole. I try to think of some of Wire's lyrics but all I can come up with is "Hale's one, the air is thin/ thick smoke in tides of blue./ Elvis has a wooden heart... "I can't think of the next line but figure it's bizarre enough to lean over and whisper

"I'd like to onomatopoeia your perineum."

The kid shrugs. "Sure, why not."

He says it the way we used to in the 70s when we were offered drugs. Or was it the 80s? In The Lizard Club, time and space melt like snowflakes.

Outside the sky's filthy with bangles but soft somehow,

and pensive like the stage directions to a Frank O'Hara play. We wait for a taxi. I'm determined to keep my mouth shut, let the kid talk, but he doesn't, not until we're in his room and he asks if I'd like to see a film he's making. This time I shrug.

"Sure, why not."

He slaps a two inch reel on his portable movie projector and flicks the switch. A couple girls are talking (they're either sisters or long lost friends) and some guy comes in and the girl on the right tells him to fuck off. Then he puts on another reel of the same scene only with everyone naked. "If I were the sphinx, airplanes would veer off course and crash when I smiled," says the girl in the movie. The kid says he's going to edit the two reels together. He's reaching for a third reel when I reach over and grab him.

"Whadaya say *we* get naked?"

Without answering the kid slips out of his clothes, letting me see his naked body before he turns off the light. In the dark his body is a ghostly white but I know it's real when I bite his neck, squeeze his nipples, and pull him over to me. He slaps against me like an electrical storm. My teeth, tongue, and fingers knead his flesh, thrusting him into landscapes he's never felt before—savage, fiery landscapes of the late Jurassic period. His second brain, the brain in his tail is activated now and he shudders spasmodically, cries out in pain and pleasure as I carry him to new heights. He slams against me, pulls back when my teeth fasten on his left pectoral. My right hand slaps his raised buttocks like a thunderclap.

For a few seconds I let him catch his breath—no touch at all—then gently massage the back of his neck and flutter my fingers lightly over his chest. My right little fingernail zips down his left side fast, reckless as a kid on a skateboard.

Back and forth, from sisterly tenderness to Jurassic fury, till the boy's utterly addled and comes at me with the blind lust of a diplodocus. His cock finds my mouth, stabbing at it

59

wildly, until I stick a finger up his ass so as to better conduct this erotic symphony. With my other hand I pinch and pull at his nipples, squeeze his balls, and play with his perineum.

O perineum, perambulating between anus and cock, you are my Gaza Strip, my Yellow Brick Road, my Great Wall of China. How I worship you! How I adore your hairy pores and delicate ridges! I lick and nibble there with Hansel and Gretel and lo, though my tongue wanders through the Valley of Death, I shall not want. For you are my Good Shepherd, my Ariadne's thread, my *Bridge Over the River Kwai* (which won seven Academy Awards but deserved more). You lead me from the murky depths to the shining lighthouse, from the sulfurous pit to Mount Olympus. You make the blind see, the lame walk, and when I give you a little jiggle the whole universe moves. O treasure guarded by dragons! O key to the music of the spheres! O sweet perineum, deliver me from mine enemies, now and at the hour of my little death!

Then, with lizardlike speed, I slip on a condom and flip the kid over. I enter him like the Huns did Rome. I plough into him like that blazing meteor which plunged into the Caribbean Sea sixty-five million years ago causing great tidal waves, earthquakes, and a nuclear winter that finished off the dinosaurs (or was it volcanos that knocked them off?). I'm still jerking him off as I fuck him. He's so out of it now he doesn't even notice when I slip my lips over his head and suck up his final remains.

In the morning I awake exhausted. The room is a wreck, but so it was to start with—clothes, books, empty beer cans everywhere. I pick up a tape of Mabel Mercer singing Cole Porter (not what I'd have expected to find) and shove it into the tape deck. As Mabel croons "It was the *wrrong* face, in the *wrrong* place" (rolling her r's in a corny French accent), I wander from room to room eating the kid's roommates one by one. It was a very Pelagian morning.

-7-

THE SAURIAN RECOVERY LEAGUE

"Hello, Maddy?"

"Steve, what's up?"

"Well, I'm in this apartment on Oak Street and I'm having a little trouble. I just ate everyone here and now I can't squeeze out the door."

Maddy and Tom drove over in their battered 64 VW van with the Micky and Minnie Mouse stickers on the back and, after basting me liberally with Wesson oil, they managed to push, pull, and pry me through the door with the aid of two cookie sheets. It took about forty-five minutes and I was pretty embarrassed, so when Maddy once again suggested that I attend a meeting with them, I agreed.

The Saurian Recovery League met in the basement of a Salvation Army used clothing store in the Outer Mission. Luckily it had a coal chute, because I was still too bloated to get down the narrow stairway. Tumble-bumpity-bump-BLAT, and I'm heaped on the floor looking up at ten or fifteen lizards sprawled around a big wooden table. The room smelled dank and clammy, with cardboard boxes of old clothes stacked against one wall and hand lettered signs saying JUST DON'T TAKE THE FIRST BITE, IT'S NUTS TO EAT PEOPLE, and GET SERIOUS! thumbtacked on the other. A list of the League's Nine Precepts was posted next to the stairs. Someone gave me a copy of it after the meeting.

★ ★ ★ ★ ★

1) We admit to the voraciousness of our appetites, which has addled our brains and made our tails unmanageable.

2) We came to believe that a power greater than ourselves could restore us to sanity.

3) We ask this cosmic power to either do so, or to return us to the tar pits where we belong.

4) We agree to check out where our heads are at.

5) We admit to ourselves and to other lizards the exact nature of our hallucinations.

6) We humbly ask Taricheas (or whatever other god, goddess or Buddha nature will listen) to remove our unappeasable saurian appetites.

7) We agree to make restitution wherever possible, except when to do so would horrify others.

8) We specifically agree to try *NOT* to:
   a) penetrate the souls of others with our eyes,
   b) stick out or wag our tongues lasciviously,
   c) detach or thrash our tails in public.
   d) puff ourselves up grotesquely or squirt blood from our eyes,
   e) play loud rock music or engage in other behavior that might instigate saurian behavior in others,
   f) eat people or any other meat not properly processed, packaged, and approved by proper government authorities.

9) Having sloughed off our old skins as a result of practicing these precepts, we will carry our transmogrification to any other suffering saurians who care to listen.

★ ★ ★ ★ ★

The meeting began with the secretary, a cute little iguana named Connie, welcoming everyone. "We don't care what kind of people you're used to eating," Connie began. "Just don't brag about it. We have no time for ego tripping or theological debates. The Saurian Recovery League has no dues or fees but there's a can in back to pay for cookies and coffee. You're a member when you say you are. If you think you've eaten anyone in the last twenty-four hours, please don't talk during the meeting, but stay afterwards and get phone numbers. 'A lizard alone needs a telephone,' as we say.

"As for today's topic—well, I've been thinking a lot about insanity lately. I've been coming to these meetings for over a year and, even though I haven't eaten anyone, I still feel like a lizard. When's it gonna stop? I mean is it my hairstyle or what? Anyway, you can talk about whatever you want, but I'd like to hear what you do when you're feeling crazy. Jean?"

A slender fringe-tailed lizard in a black leather jacket was the first to speak.

"My name is Jean and I'm a recovering lizard. Thanks, Connie. Your topic hits the nail right on the tail for me, cuz on weekends I want to be out having fun but I don't know how to do that except by eating people. I can't even go to a cafe or grocery store without thinking about it. Like there's this cute guy who lives downstairs from me who has a Harley. Every weekend he's out in the drive working on it with his shirt off. His pecs just drive me crazy. So I came here. I mean it was either that or go to Bakers Beach again and swim under the sand."

"Thanks Jean. You're in the right place. Lamont?"

"Ya, I got some money in the bank," says a shabbily dressed collared lizard in back. He mumbles, and talks so fast it's hard to catch everything he says. "That means I gotta

63

deal with the bank and I hate it. Then my upstairs neighbors have been persecuting me and calling me a chameleon—'Cham the Sham,' their kids call me. But what's worse is they play the radio real loud, reruns of these old shows like "The Green Hornet" and "The Shadow." "The Green Hornet" starts with "Flight of the Bumblebee" which I just hate: all this buzz-buzz, death stalks the city, the Green Hornet strikes again!!! And the Shadow is named Lamont, just like me. He travelled to the Orient and learned how to cloud people's minds with his hypnotic power so they can't see him. I'm afraid that the people upstairs know who I really am—Lamont Cranston, millionaire playboy and crusader against evil. I think I should eat them to protect my identity, but first I have to see my shrink and tell him I don't want to see him anymore cuz the medication he prescribes for me is actually..."

"Thank you, Lamont."

"Who knows what evil *lurks* in the hearts of men? The *Shadow* knows. HAHAHAHAHAHA!" (Lamont laughs weirdly.)

"*Thank* you, Lamont."

"But for the newcomers, keep coming to meetings every day, stay away from rock concerts and clubs..."

Lamont was talking so fast now that he was barely comprehensible. For an instant he looked like an ordinary crack addict, such as you see in the Tenderloin, and I wondered if my own perception of these people as lizards was merely *my* craziness. Maybe I didn't really eat anyone on Oak Street after all? Maybe all this was just a horrible dream, or the result of a psychotic break caused by Squirmy's leaving me? Then I heard Maddy's voice—shy, tentative, soothing.

"Insanity for me starts when I get up in the morning. I might be on this pink cloud singing and all and then I have to go to work and I think, '*Shit*! I might as well be dead.' I haven't done *anything* with my life, and if I take classes at

State again I'm afraid I'll fuck up like I did last time. That red-baiting instructor made me so mad I couldn't help it."

"And another thing," Lamont interrupts. "My neighbors are persecuting me with their dog who's always sniffing at my door. Is it a slip to eat dogs?"

"Don't interrupt, Lamont. Maddy has the floor now."

"Well, that's all I wanted to say really," Maddy laughs shyly. "I'm just grateful to be coming here is all. I've lost a lot of weight for one thing. So whenever I feel crazy I make a list of things I'm grateful for."

Next to speak was a skinny Gila Monster with thick nerdy glasses and a red baseball cap which he had on backwards. He said he joined the League because of his anxiety attacks. He wasn't technically schizophrenic, he said, but whenever he looked at people he imagined their heads exploding in clouds of pink gore. He said he had a friend who believed nervous breakdowns were good for you, but when he started to tell his friend that he disagreed, he opened his mouth so wide that his friend freaked out.

(All the lizards laughed at this. In fact, I noticed that the weirder and more horrifying the comments, the more they laughed. What a jovial crew!)

The skinny kid said he later wondered if he'd just hallucinated this cuz he watched a lot of David Cronenberg movies like *Scanners* and *Videodrome*. Scanners were psychics who could make people's heads explode. Anyway, the kid said he was feeling a lot less crazy since he'd stopped watching so many horror movies (although he had one slip when he rented the home video of *Brain Damage*).

"I'm really glad to have these meetings," someone named John said next, "but I wish I had someone I could invite over to dinner. I used to do that a lot before I came into the League, but I ate all my dinner guests. Now nobody

65

wants to come to dinner any more, even though I'm a really good cook.

"What I mean, I guess, is that I think my craziness comes from being alone too much. When I was really young I started listening to the voice of God. God told me to be His prophet, to say no to drugs, and to return the earth to the purity of the Jurassic era. Later, when I started highschool, I just waited for the bombs to fall or for civilization to collapse so I could play in the ruins. With everything falling apart, I figured it wouldn't matter if I ate a few people. I was just doing my bit to control the world's population. Now I realize I just wanted to get high—about three stories high, like a Tyrannosaurus. Face it, eating someone is a rush! We wouldn't do it otherwise.

"But since joining the League I don't have so much indigestion. I mean some of the people I ate were really nasty. They smoked, drank, did drugs, ate sugar and food with all kinds of weird chemicals in it, had toxic livers, and used all kinds of sprays and lotions on their hair and skin. They also had fingernail polish on, snot hanging out of their noses—you eat all that shit and you're a mess."

The last speaker was an older basilisk with baggy circles under his eyes. I gather from how respectfully everyone listened that he'd been in the League for some time.

"Hi, my name's Bob and I'm a recovering lizard. I've heard a lot of good stuff here today. Like John said, when you eat people, you can't help but feel crazy because the stuff in their systems changes your thinking process in a physical way. I mean, you can cook up some really twisted world views and it takes years, even after you're in recovery, to totally detox. So when I used to eat someone just to change the way I felt, *that* was insanity. And I know with me, it had a lot to do with low self esteem.

"So it's not surprising we still feel crazy. I know I do. Even after ten years in the League. And violence—I get the feeling all the time that I'd like to get a machine gun and blow away some cops, or yuppie landlord scum, or cars that try to run me down on Market Street. That's natural, but it's also true that I want to blame everything outside of me for how I feel inside.

"Like today, some nice old ladies were trying to get on the elevator and I was trying to shut the door in their faces because I was late for an appointment. I could tell that they thought I was trying to keep the door open for them. What I wanted to scream was, 'Fuck you! Can't you see I'm trying to close this damn door in your faces and get away from you?'

"And that's okay. Everyone feels that way sometimes. The difference is that today I don't have to eat someone over it. Instead I work the Saurian League precepts, especially the first four. That's what keeps my insanity from overwhelming me, that and these meetings. These meetings are the only place we can be totally honest and let our tails hang out. You know, some lizards have so much denial that if I scuttled in here covered from head to toe in shit, they'd say, 'My Bob, you look really good in brown. Goes so well with your alligator shoes.' But that's not what we're about here. We're into honesty.

"So if you're new to the League and didn't hear anything you can identify with today, keep coming back. You'll hear your story eventually."

Afterwards, everyone joined hands and recited the Saurian League mantra. I can't recall it exactly, but it went something like this: "Taricheas, grant us the strength to transform the icy patches of our planet, the serenity to accept the civilized parts, and the wisdom to know the difference."

67

I was feeling better already. In fact, with a little effort I was even able to squeeze upstairs, instead of having to be pulled up the coal chute.

-8-

FROM LEX ICON TO COUNT LESARD

Maddy, Tom, Lex, and I stop in at the Neo Hip Retro 50s Diner on 9th and Folsom. "Wow," Tom enthuses. "This booth is made outta real pseudo vinyl naugahyde. And look at these menus encased in **Green Jello** laminate."

"What'll it be folks?" inquires the automaton waitress in a Marge Simpson beehive.

"I'll have the **Strawberry Alarm Clock** Mousse with diced chiggers on the side," Maddy says.

"Make mine the Fried Bavarian Eggshells over the **Gene Spliced Meal Worms**," Tom adds. "And I'd like some **Smokin' Rhythm Prawns** too."

Lex orders **Lubricated Goat** in **Monks of Doom** sauce. I can't decide what to get. I hate dining in restaurants, but if I have to I might as well order something I wouldn't ordinarily fix at home, like **Fish and Roses**. It's a Thai dish made with **Mighty Lemon Drops**, **Virgin Prunes**, and **Dead Milkmen** (oops! I mean **Red Hot Chili Peppers**.). Tastes great with Thai **Ice-T**, but if you eat too much you have to call the **Medicine Men**.

Actually, this is just a coded rundown of a few bands we like. Lex is a DJ and sometimes we talk in code about what's happening on the music/heresy front. After my culinary debauch of the night before, I decide to stick with the light citrus bands so when the waitress returns I order a Waldorf salad of **Moby Grape, Bananarama,** and **Tangerine Dream**. My mom used to make this as a topping over **Vanilla Fudge**.

"Apollinaire was a great gourmet," Lex says. "When he became a poet and was too poor to eat he tortured himself recalling his favorite childhood dishes: fircone kernels roasted over a fire, orange-rind dragees and aniseed balls, pancakes made of peach paste. Once he and Alfred Jarry drank absinthe mixed with red ink so that later their piss would be red."

(Lex is not really telling me about the nineteenth century French Surrealist poet but about Apollinarius, the anti-Arian Bishop of Laodicea and tutor of Saint Jerome who said that Christ had a human body and emotions but a divine soul. This made Christ a hybrid mutant. Pope Damasus condemned Apollinarius for this and, after several synods and the Council of Constantinople declared these ideas *anathema sit* in A.D. 381, our old friend Theodosius brought in the force of secular law. But is laconic Lex comparing this heresy to our own homosaurian condition and warning me against the Saurian League's theology, or is he just being a smartass? I turn the topic of conversation back to music to see if I can find out.)

"That reminds me of my uncle Leonard," I say. "He told the same joke every Fourth of July. 'Don't eat that watermelon! It's sick. It has blood in its urine.' Then he'd sit down to play The Meatmen's 'Tooling for Anus' on the piano."

"I bet that set your great aunt's feet a tappin.'"

"It sure did, although my parents missed the humor of it. How'd you become a DJ anyway?"

"Well, I created my first alter-identity in college when I did a talk show on this bogus campus radio station where the signal went through electricity in the dorms. I kept getting kicked off one station and going to another cuz the people I interviewed used obscenities. Then when I moved out here I did a show on KALX, the UC Berkeley station. I did more music then but interviewed performance artists and bands like the Volcano Suns."

"Whadaya think of the Lounge Lizards?"

"They're great! Jazz with a bite, not abrasive like Industrial but not overly melodic either. Not mindless decoration wallpaper music like Oingo Boingo who do have a song 'Reptiles and Samauri' and use slides of lizards in their shows but they're so dorky. It's like air-freshener to cover up the silence. The Lounge Lizards give a more genuine saurian sensibility even without lyrics."

"What about The Church? They have a reptile song too on their *Starfish* album."

"Well, they've been around for awhile. They're sorta like The Smiths."

"Remember The Flying Lizards in the 70s?" Maddy interjects.

"Ya, and don't forget Culture Club's 'Karma Chameleon,'" Tom adds. To prove his pop expertise, he sings the chorus: "'Karma karma karma karma karma karma karma cham-eel-eon...'"

"Boy George was a chameleon alright," Lex replies, "but the only group to do a really *good* lizard song, besides Shriek Path, The Pelagians, and maybe Siouxsie and the Banshees group New Creatures, who did that song 'Gecko,' is the Doors' 'Celebration of the Lizard.' Jim Morrison had some good stuff in his *New Creatures* poems too: 'Soft lizard eyes connect' or 'Lizard woman/ With your insect eyes/ With your wild surprise/ Warm daughter of silence/ Venom/ Turn your back with a slither of moaning wisdom.' Morrison was The Lizard King." Lex's eyes glaze over in euphoric nostalgia.

Telepathically, I can hear him pulling up Morrison's rich, resonant voice, his shifts in rhythm and discourse against the ominous rattles and organ arpeggios. Something about Morrison's voice was definitely prehistoric—erotic yet scary— like the echoing challenge of a primal dream or a gecko's shadow slithering over a rock:

> Try this little game of going insane
> deep into the brain past the realm of pain....
> not to touch the earth, not to see the sun
> nothing to do but run, run, run...

Then the deafening, drunken roar of the crowd yelling "More, more," when the song's finished.

"The 70s—that's the last time I can remember feeling I was really on top of what was happening musically," Tom agrees.

"You guys are just confusing Steve," Maddy objects. "Our Saurian League motto is 'Keep it simple,' remember? If you want to find out how we started, Steve, forget Jim Morrison and all these Johnny-come-latelys. Read the first fifty pages of *The Green Book* by Count Lesard."

"Count Lesard?"

"Tall, skinny guy. Doesn't go out much," Lex smirks.

Maddy glares, then fills me in. "He thought up the League's Nine Precepts over one hundred years ago and explains in his book how to work them. He includes saurian history, adages, and prophesies, you name it. If you want, I'll loan you my copy."

Tom pays for our meal with his Telecredit Card and we slide down the travel chute to the van. He, Maddy and Lex are going to the Open Rant at Klubstitute but they drop me off on the way. Maddy loans me her *Green Book* which I begin to read when I get up to my apartment.

THE GREEN BOOK

By Count Lesard

I was born in 1850 in a haunted mansion in the isolated, swampy region of Medoc, France. I am told that when my mother saw me she gave a scream and expired. Whether this is true or not I don't know, but I was subsequently raised by an aged uncle who was blind and deaf and therefore more understanding.

Three things distinguished me: my scaly skin and saurian nature, my uncanny ability to remember the future instead of the past, and my ability to read people's minds. By the age of four I surmised from scanning my uncle's mind that our family had descended from the great ninth century Bogomile, Pop Jeremiah, who compiled Christian apocryphal legends such as *The Legend of the Cross*. The Bogomiles were dualists who believed that Christ and Satan were twins. After Satan rebelled and was expelled from heaven, Christ was sent to destroy his power by bringing Adam's seed back to heaven. Unlike the Cathars, we Bogomiles had no qualms about prevaricating in order to escape persecution. By the fouteenth century we had merged with more libertine sects, and my family immigrated to France. One forbearer, Henri Lesard VI, had the misfortune to become astrologer to the black magician and boy killer Giles de Rais and perished with him at the stake. But the main branch of our family became respected merchants, trading in rare furs and precious gems.

But while I can tell you my family history from reading my uncle's mind, I can't tell you what I had yesterday for breakfast. Which is perhaps just as well, considering my preferred diet.

As for my lizard nature, it did not seem any more remarkable to me than the fact that Venus flytraps consume flesh, that birds evolved from Dinosaurs, or that tuataras have a third eye on top of their heads. Our world is a most astonishing place and as Isidore of Seville wrote in his *Etymologie*, the word monster (*monstrum*) derives from *demonstrare*, meaning to show or demonstrate. Heresy and evolutionary change are thus mere intrusions into a homogeneous perception of reality. *My* vocation, I decided, would be to make my life an example.

But of what?

This question became my all-consuming passion, and I began researching what had been written about lizards over the years. Not much. The only biblical reference, in *Leviticus*, states that we are "unclean." Pliny, in his *Natural History* (A.D. 77), said that basilisks can kill by smell or looks. Subsequent bestiaries added allegorical Christian morals, but remained confused as to what distinguishes us from snakes and dragons. Ovid didn't mention us at all in his *Metamorphoses,* and subsequent western writers (Shakespeare, etc.) refer to us only in passing.

Moving East, we were treated only slightly more favorably. In Egypt we were thought to rejuvenate the old, and the *Rubaiyat of Omar Khayyam* states, "They said the lion and lizard keep/ the courts where Jamshyd gloried and drank deep...." Arabians believed a lizard held in the hand acts as an aphrodisiac, and in India we were used as good luck charms.

But, as usual, we were often lumped together with serpents and dragons. Persians and Indians considered the *naga* snake holy, a rain and water deity which became in China the raging *chiao* dragon. In the eighth century, this dragon regularly assumed human shape. Chinese folk literature abounds with tales of women who, after bathing in rivers, give birth to dragon children who later become great kings. In a ninth century story a widow finds five dragon eggs and acquires miraculous powers along with the title "Mother of Dragons."

Moving farther east, the Aranda of Australia believed that we drew the first humans out of the ocean. If anyone killed us, the sky would crush the earth. On the Malay Peninsula we infused babies with souls. Melanesians also believe dream-souls assume saurian form. In Tahiti we're the "shadow of the gods," and in Polynesia people worship Moko, the lizard king.

But China, Tahiti, and Polynesia are far from France and I soon learned, once I got beyond my uncle's protection, that if I wished to survive I would have to employ more than clairvoyance. So at the age of seven I chose the first of my alter-identities—Odilon Redon. I was the child who wore black, who drew spiders with human faces. I decided to show how illusory boundaries are and to demonstrate Thomas Mann's dictum that time and space "slip away like a lizard, smooth and faithless." I would be the first artist of total transgression.

All day I worked on my drawings and lithographs. Then, in the early evening, I would step out on the balcony to watch, rising at the east end of the Mountains of the Tripdars, the river flowing into the gloomy forest of the Horibs through which it runs down to the Rela Am, or River of Darkness. Edgar Rice Burroughs writes of this a hundred years later. Countless writers would be struck by the majesty of our grounds. William Burroughs, for instance, would be impressed by the phallic trees rising out of the swamp, and by how unbearably erotic the whole landscape is at twilight. Sometimes I would project a mishmash of these yet-to-be-written texts into the minds of servants and friends so that I could have the pleasure of hearing them acted out.

* * * * *

HORIB (PLAYED BY PETER THE STABLEBOY): We
        take you to our village where you will be well f
        You cannot escape us; no one escapes the Hori

(Tarzan hesitates. The Red Flower of Zoram moves
closer to his side.)

RED FLOWER OF ZORAM (PLAYED BY MARIE THE
        MAID): (Whispers) Let us go with them. We cani
        escape them now; there are too many of them.

(From my hiding place I watch her lips approach
Tarzan's red flower, *their softest touch as smart as
lysards' stings*, which in the dying sunlight showed a
brilliant catamite red.)

TARZAN (PLAYED BY JOHN MARSTON): Thou foggie
        dulnesse, speake: lives not more faith in a home
        thrusting tongue than in these fencing tip tap
        courtiers?

RED FLOWER OF ZORAM: Beware of a facile moral,
        Tarzan.

(This I assume she adds for the benefit of Tarzan's
accompanist, a young nun with a face like some stra
white rock who was inclined to give herself married
airs, since she had been debauched, one otiose noor
by a demon.)

TARZAN: If I recollect, the last time I preached was c
        the theme of flagellation, a sermon I propose to
        publish.

HORIB: (Now that he has recognized the other prisoi
        ers) Well for Pity sakes! I have learned to look w
        comparative composure upon wooly rhinoceros
        mammoths, trachodons, and pterodactyls but I
        never expected to see Captain Kidd, Lafitte, anc
        Henry Morgan in the heart of Pellucidar.

CAPTAIN KIDD (PLAYED BY BAUDELAIRE): Hope, th
        never forsak'st the wretchedst man yet bidst m
        live and lurke in this disguise.

LAFFITE (PLAYED BY RIMBAUD): People won't com
        one in a peach-charmeuse trimmed with po

One requires moonstones, veils, and a ghoul-
ish cut to one's skirt. It's so tiresome not to be
able to wear one's professional clothes in the
street.

NATIVE BEARERS (PLAYED BY SUNDRY OTHER
SERVANTS): (Referring both to the Horibs and the
pirates) We'll try most anything once, suh, but not
dem babies.

★ ★ ★ ★ ★

The fact that these spontaneous skits made no
logical sense is what most appealed to me. Theater like
a jungle! Characters, themes, speeches, images arising
from nowhere like swamp gas and then, just as suddenly,
disappearing as if zapped by a chameleon's tongue.
"Every man worthy of the part has a lizard in his heart," as
Baudelaire once remarked. And it was true. Both visually
and in these skits I captured the brutal evolutionary
rhythms of life.

Then, at age twenty, I discovered *Maldoror* by
Count Lautreamont. Rimbaud and I were furious.
Lautreamont hurled forward as if into a mouth devouring
both space and time. Even his flowers drew humans
"toward a cave of hell." No wonder he punctuated each
sentence as he declaimed it by pounding a piano chord.
His poetry possessed the speed and fury of music—or *noise*
as it's always first called. Lautreamont not only wrote
about but *was* the black hole to which Rimbaud and I
aspired.

Rimbaud's response, as usual, was petulant. « *Je
suis l'autre*, » he announced defiantly, meaning, "I *am*
Lautreamont," or "*I* was here first." For while Lautreamont
was only writing about the teeth of lice, Rimbaud was
pulling them from his hair and throwing them at cafe
patrons. And while Lautreamont wrote of the claw and
sucker, Rimbaud was literally clawing and sucking Verlaine
away from his wife.

My own response was more complex. While I envied
Lautreamont's swollen aggressivity, I could not help
but notice the rarity of saurians in his bestiary:

basilisks and vipers seldom appeared, and
Lautreamont's eagle tears into the dragon "like a
leech... until his whole neck is in the dragon's stomach."
But when Lautreamont describes his flying octopus, I could
not help but marvel—especially at the screams of its
victims: "[the screams] were transformed into vipers
as they came out of his mouth and ran to hide in the
underbrush, among ruined walls, luring day and night.
These screams, creeping along and endowed with
innumerable coils, small flattened heads, and treacher-
ous eyes, have sworn to take a stand before human
innocence."

Here was a cruelty to admire. So while Rimbaud
fled from the field of battle and went to Brussels with
Verlaine, I decided to confront Lautreamont directly.

What a nerd he was in person—tall and skinny
with a high, squeaky voice. All his transgressiveness was
mental, whereas I...well, to shorten my story I easily
seduced him and soon swallowed and digested
everything he had to offer. Until now, my diet had
consisted mainly of stray cats and dogs with an
occasional peasant or schoolboy thrown in for variety.
But with the ingestion of Lautreamont, my appetite
for human flesh became insatiable. Bloated from one
meal, I would force myself to regurgitate so that I could
indulge in another. Night and day I thought of nothing
else. My art, my studies, my couture and my health
suffered greatly as a result.

* * * * *

At this point I began to doze. Count Lesard was apparently
another lizard who never knew when to shut up. Maybe I'd
find out how he hit upon his nine noble precepts tomorrow.
For now, exhausted from tewnty-four hours of gustatory
pyrotechnics and trying to follow the circumlocutions first of
the Saurian Recovery League meeting and then of Lex Icon
and Count Lesard, I began to drift off to the Land of Nod.

–9–

THE KLUBSTITUTE DREAM

In my dream there were seven fat cows and seven skinny cows and they all went down to Klubstitute to drink. It was a dull night—no heretics about—but the Red Flower of Zoram had merged with Squirmy to become Omewenne, a diaphanous beauty of uncertain gender. S\He was singing old Borborite love songs acapella: one voice miaowing like a Hawaian gecko, the other spacious and mournful as a school of humpback whales.

> *Kooo-Khoooah! Khoooah!*
> Splash! Miaow, miaow!

Maybe Omewenne is my higher power? A soft mossy reincarnation of Mishima's *Kurotokage* (*Black Lizard*), androgynous shadows and light flickering against the movie screen of my inner eyelids? If only we could always be adored like this. O radiance! O celery terriaki! O peacock feather on the tip of your green claw!

Now I notice we're at the bottom of the sea, for Jerome swims by wearing ripped fishnet stockings and with a hologram of her beating heart tatooed beneath her irridescent green bra. "Everyone's doing the best they can," she murmurs, swishing onto a pot of gold. Her breath rises to the surface in cartoon air bubbles.

In my dream Kenneth Anger becomes Carmen Miranda, and Rimbaud and Verlaine finally work it out. The astrophysicist Stephen Hawking comes in and says, "There's no hair on this black hole." We don't know what he means exactly but maybe it's this: remember how your dog's legs sometimes vibrated while he slept and mom said, "Sparkie's just dreaming of chasing rabbits"? Imagine a herd of Archosaurs dreaming!

-10-

READING LIZARD PROVERBS TO SEAN

Sunday morning!

I can never hear these words without thinking of Nico's cold sweet voice commingling with the little bells in that first Velvet Underground record, the one where a yellow banana skin peels off revealing a luscious pink fruit underneath. But today I awake in a panic. I feel I've just eaten not only the seven skinny cows but also the seven fat ones and everyone else at Klubstitute too.

"It's just a lizard dream," Maddy says when I call her. "We often dream we eat people when we get into recovery. Seems so real, huh."

Maddy suggests I take a brisk walk, so I race down the three flights of stairs and out onto 16th Street to view the new graffitti and posters: PLAN AHEAD (image of George Bush with Dan Quale wart growing out of his forehead), SAFE (tongue approaching a nipple), INTRODUCTION TO CHEROTIC MAGIC FOR WARRIORS WHO WANT TO GO INTO TABOO AREAS, TO PUSH BEYOND WHERE IT'S COMFORTABLE & SAFE, flyers announcing bands, poetry readings, plays, etc. Layers of paper an inch thick cover some buildings—San Francisco's attempt at structural reinforcement to protect against earthquakes. Over one wall of flyers is graffittied: THE WALLS OF THE CITY SPEAK.

I decide to visit Sean SP and look at his new videos.

He was telling me about his favorites at Club Uranus where he does coat check: *Total World Liquidation Sale* and *Tommorrow* about a political activist who gets dosed at a party and turns catatonic. Sean makes videos for his weekly *Too Real TV* show on Channel 25.

Sean lives in the Outer Mission. You have to negotiate your way between Nam Yoho Renge Kyo Buddhists and crack dealers to get to his flat. His hair is wet when I arrive, and he has a video on of someone reading a dictionary definition of obscentiy over Gregorian Chant music while a guy in a suit reading a magazine exclaims "Naked! Exposed!" afterwhich the camera pans pictures of deforestation.

"I did this one in response to all the critical mail I got over 'Honey, I'm Home,' which showed someone shooting up shit out of a toilet," Sean says. "I guess that video is the best example of something I've done where I asked myself 'Why did you make this?' afterwards. I don't feel any responsibility for showing society's ugliness, because that's what's there. I want to make people think about their lives. Most TV just entertains people."

I ask Sean what he thinks about lizards, something we've never talked about before. He says he thinks they're scarey cuz they don't have emotions and they're so calculated and efficient, and because of how they jump around so quickly.

"I was on mushrooms at a party in North Beach," Sean says. "I saw this lizard sitting on the TV so I forced myself to pet it to overcome my fear. But lizards don't enjoy being touched as much as mammals do."

Then Sean confesses he had a chameleon and a salamander awhile back and that he liked watching them eat crickets. I notice his face is generally as expressionless as track lighting in a downtown office, except when he talks about his videos, whereupon he becomes vivaciously childlike. He moves his arms around a lot too, mostly reaching under the sleeves of his faded red tee-shirt to scratch. Then he'll suddenly jump up to snap a new video into the VCR. Sean is wearing cut-offs. I'd like to pet him or touch his furry leg but get the feeling he wouldn't like it, even though he's obstensibly a mammal. We smoke some dope. I don't know if I'd call Sean calculating or efficient, but I guess he is capable enough to pay his rent and get his videos done for his show each week. Otherwise I wouldn't be here watching this stuff.

"I loved watching *Star Trek* and *Kung Fu* on TV when I was a kid," Sean continues, steering the conversation back to his favorite topic. "I loved the monastery flashbacks where the Kung Fu guy remembers these little moral lessons. In *Star Trek* I liked how they projected contemporary problems into the future, so people could look at them without their usual prejudices. Like once they go to this planet made out of LSD and get fried."

Sean uses a lot of extreme close-ups cuz he likes to fill the whole screen. This stretches and distorts his actors' faces. He likes using images, color, and political rap poems he writes too, which he memorizes after reading them three or four times. But he especially likes video because you "can force people to take a different perspective on life than they usually would because the camera is subjective."

How would one do a video showing the world from a saurian perspective?

Imagine a touching love story between an old lizard and a young boy. The boy, who never looks into the eyes of another human, spends hours staring into the eyes of his lizard. Just staring into someone's eyes for a long time is psychic. At first it's very strange and scary—scarier than the first time you have sex. Then you begin to relax, and the person you're

83

looking at may become very beautiful. As you look into their eyes you may see them change sex or age or race. You can see the child in an old person and a young person may appear ancient. Just looking into someone's eyes for a long time can be trippier than taking acid.

"Why are you doing a book on lizards," Sean asks. "Is it because you feel like one?"

"I don't know. I don't remember why I started, but once I did it just seemed to keep going. I guess I want people to take a different perspective, like you do in your videos. Have you ever heard of the great saurian heretic Count Lesard?"

Sean hasn't. I show him *The Green Book*, in particular a section entitled "Prophesies and Proverbs." Sean asks what a heretic is. I tell him it's someone who rejects mainstream religious beliefs. He asks what a proverb is. I say it's like the moral lessons in the monastery flashbacks on *Kung Fu*. Then I open *The Green Book* and read a few of the proverbs to him.

★ ★ ★ ★ ★

THE PROPHESIES AND PROVERBS OF COUNT LESARD

1. The higher the altitude, the less concentrated the lizard population. No Swiss Alps clarity for us! We prefer the fetid jungle, the convoluted text, the dark pits & valleys of the groin.
2. A slip of the tongue, a flick of a wrist, a wink of an eye— seduction lulls with perfidious enchantments. Saurians likewise mark their turf with a combination of sudden movement and disappearance.
3. What constitutes a slip of the tongue? Bad timing, good breeding, or the engine of the unconscious? We lizards say, "Fuck guilt!"

4. Gut instinct, I know in my gut it's true, etc. Few humans can swallow a truth whole; fewer still can digest it. Saurians are the only true philosphers of "the real."

5. Slide into pleasure, eviscerate meaning.

6. How long *is* a brontosaurus's gut anyway, or a story with no plot, no character, no end?

7. Lizards are accused of being unfeeling but we could never be as rapacious as humans. Tyrannosaurus Rex killed only when hungry. Human despots (Caligula, Idi Amin) kill for sport; faceless bureaucrats (Napoleon, George Bush, etc.) kill from boredom or to compensate for masculine insecurities.

    So don't condemn Henry Kissinger, George Shultz, or Jesse Helms for their "saurian girth," their "reptilian expressions," their "cold lizard eyes" and "forked tongues." It's their *humanity* that is repulsive.

8. Why will Jean Baudrillard be called the lizard of philosophy? In a time when consumerism reigns he will glory in having pushed thought into an ecological niche where he can pick and nibble at it, while peeking out at the future from under a rock.

9. For fear of thirst we chose swamps, for fear of hunger we chose teeth, for fear of madness we chose death. Before man and god were invented the world was a happier place.

10. Why does he talk to me? Why does he flit away? Look deep enough into the universe and you'll see the back of your own head.

11. A dog wagging its tail does not appreciate Beethoven. A lizard smacking its lips doesn't mean that this is a four star restaurant.

12. Favorite dish in Chinese restaurant: Sum Yung Boy.

13. Sucking his cock made me forget the future. Losing him nailed me to the past.

14. Leaning over a thousand-year-old lake, an ancient tree propped up by crutches. This is how passion

looks to those who've never known anything but passing whims.

15. "Scary, but fun," OR "scary butt fun?" On the saurian scales of justice, slime is no crime.

16. Humans: kiss and tell.
Lizards: eat and run.
Homosaurians: we want it *all*!

17. People ask what I think of punk rock. O retreads of Nervous Norvus, neckties of Nerval! Those who pierce their cheeks with safety pins are still playing it too safe.

18. If you're afraid to dive into the void, either ask for a shove or get off the diving board.

19. The desperate kiss of a dying child, a butterfly landing on an asphixated flower. Such cries fall backwards in the wind. Instead, shout greetings to those invisible forms we're evolving towards.

20. The reverse is also true: ghosts could not have existed without us.

21. No apology, no retreat, no more pussyfooting with the Powers That Be.

22. The shortest verses of the Bible are "Jesus wept" and "Lazarus laughed." But *why* did Lazarus laugh? Because he thought being called back to life was a joke? Or was he still laughing from the riotous comedy he'd witnessed in hell?

23. The ultimate heresy: any and all belief separates one from direct experience and is therefore *anathema*.

24. Nietzsche refers to "tedious frogs crawling and hopping around and inside men as if they were as thoroughly at home there as in a swamp." What a splendid description, and one to be extended. Imagine the decomposition of food stewing in digestive juices, putrid gasses rising in the intestines, fecal matter skateboarding toward the anus. Who doesn't live this way today? But how exciting to be living amongst a doomed species in a society

so stagnant that phosphorous vapors flare up like a halo over a corpse. One can only marvel.

25. An army of sixteen-year-olds is terrifying; but our souls are one hundred and sixty million years old and loom up before you more terrifying still.

26. Slinking toward the millenium: in the 40s, class; in the 60s, sass; in the 80s, crass. What does humanity have left to devour except itself?

27. A cannibalistic society has no unconscious; an unconscious society is unaware of its origins; an unoriginal society is cannibalistic. One can only escape this tautology through death.

28. The new politics: the oblique witicism, turning the joke around. on mushrooms (e.g., morals are learned at mother's knee or some other low joint).

29. America was colonized by soldiers of fortune and religious fanatics, so why be surprised if America's concept of freedom comes to mean freedom to exploit, to own guns. Mom, flag, and apple pie will become the symbolic cover for this, since America's "freedom" is like mom's "love" (i.e. she loves us to death). But what of free speech? When America's external enemies collapse, politicians wrapped in the flag will deny its citizens even this. America will then turn on itself like a dragon eating its young.

30. Words and syllables behave as do certain lizards; they change color according to position. For instance in the middle of "heart" is "ear"; in the middle of "death," "eat." Or if you prefer a more poetic declension: grave, rave, ave.

31. Before your eyes get to the end of this sentence I'll have forgotten why I started it. Let every waking moment be this immediate.

★ ★ ★ ★ ★

Well, you get the idea. Sean does anyway. "You've got a point," he says after I read him number seven. So why does it seem I'm so distant from him even though I'm sitting right next to him in the same room? Because I'm not a vegetarian?

We talk pleasantly about some more stuff. Then I leave humming an old Borborite love song which Omewenne was singing in my dream.

> The troglodytes
> they let to grots
> the spheric ciphers sing.
> So war distended nets I draw
> this lizard drazil thing.
> And if Saint Simon sees no mists
> nor gnostic illicit songs,
> then maybe Christ will cum to us
> from saurian suckled dongs.

–11–

THE POLITICS OF ECCENTRICITY

When I was younger, I loved visiting strange people. In college I hung out with foreign students, actors, or philosophy grad students who'd worked on whaling ships. But my favorite friend was the painter and cartoonist S. Clay Wilson. Wilson lived in his parents' fruit cellar, which he'd decorated to look like a pirate's den. He turned me on to the blues of Sonny Terry and Leadbelly, and to the drawings of Aubrey Beardsley and Edmund Gorey.

Every Friday night we'd gather at Hutton's to play Monopoly, only the way we played, everyone had to come in costume. Wilson usually dressed as a Victorian slumlord (button-on collars, spats, top hat, goldheaded cane), Claussen variously appeared as a member of Mao's Red Guard or a Nazi industrialist, and I wore the black robes of a corrupt and perverse Benedictine.

One Christmas Wilson persuaded me to drive him to Ceresco, Nebraska to visit the Surrealist painter Almquist. He wanted to give Almquist a dried toad which he'd glued onto a silver belt buckle. We didn't find Almquist but I got stuck in Almquist's garage, which was filled with mummy cases. As I tried to back up the steep, icy drive, Wilson began chanting, "Between the snow and the mummy case. Between the snow and the mummy case."

Before long, I began cultivating a few eccentricities of my own. I began reading Georges Bataille, John Dee, Dostoyevsky, Meister Eckart, Jean Genet, Witold Gombrowicz, Huysmans, Kierkegaard, Pierre Klossowski, Milorad Pavic, and every weird book I could find. I'd wander in the library stacks muttering this quote from Fra Angelico: "To paint the life of Christ, you must *live* the life of Christ." If that weren't enough, my favorite garb became the tattered felt lining of my army greatcoat.

As for my physical habits, they too became more eccentric. I had always loved picking my nose and now I did so with a vengeance. I stopped bathing—the better to retain my vital body oils, so essential for one's aura—except once a month, when I'd visit a Japanese sauna. As for my saurian fixations, I've already described some of those. Lastly, whenever I walked anywhere, I would stare intently at the ground looking for that mystical light Meister Eckart and St. John of the Cross so wonderfully reported.

I'm not sure when I realized that I too had become an eccentric. Maybe it was when I lived in this mansion and wore my thirteenth century Lord-of-Council robes? Or maybe it was when young transsexuals, urchins and drug addicts began coming over because, as one said, "If I flip out or go crazy, I figure you're *one* dude who'll understand."

As I walk home from Sean's, I pass S. Clay Wilson's flat on 16th Street. The last time I visited Wilson he was as eccentric as ever, but his casket coffee table now seemed somehow tedious.

And I wondered: who benefits from the politics of eccentricity?

Under capitalism we assume that one gains *more* personality as one gains ideas, creativity, or hours spent on a psychiatrist's couch. But what if this assumption is wrong?

What if one is *more* oneself the *less* eccentric one is?

(I must rush to get to the end of this book before my eyes give out. My right eye suffers from CMV retinitis and a detached retina; the optic nerve of my left is scarred from an old case of optic retinitis. In short, I'm fast disintegrating. But first, I recall another dream:

I'm visiting Rome with my mother. She goes ahead to the hotel while I step into a museum to see a Pasolini exhibit—slabs of ceramic tiles, friezes, and sculpture glazed to look like blue-green marble. The room looks like a demented emperor's bath. For instance, on one wall a two-foot erect penis flies towards the mouth of a sleeping old man. Others show terrified crowds fleeing from an eruption of Mount Vesuvius; or maybe God's destruction of Sodom. The art is so beautiful that I can hardly tear myself from it. In the next room, decorated wood sculptures and carved friezes confront me. I'm molested by a mechanized self-portrait of the artist.

What's especially odd about this dream is that, to my knowledge, neither Pasolini nor S. Clay Wilson ever did any sculptures. And I almost never visit museums because the reality of San Francisco's streets is so much more intense, beautiful, and bizarre.)

-12-

POSTCARD FROM M. FLANAGAN

Hi Little Stevie (as in Little Stevie of The Heretics). Here is a Caravaggio painting of a partially clothed boy called *Boy Bitten by a lizard*. It just *screamed* for me to send it to you. Speaking of screaming, I'm off to Athens tomorrow to see Diamanda perform. Deutchland is badly in need of Elavil or Lithium or both. Speaking of Elavil, have you heard from Squirmy lately?

Ciao,
M. Flanagan

* * * * *

Reading this, I'm reminded of a recent Club Opium flyer which shows a naked guy dangling a lizard from his clenched teeth by its tail. This in turn reminds me of Luisa Valenzaldua's novel *The Lizard's Tail,* which isn't about lizards but about a South American dictator with three testicles who practices Black Magick. The lizard's tail is the name of his whip.

The flyer, and the reference to Squirmy, also reminds me of cartoons I used to do for Squirmy on the backs of flyers. I no longer had Squirmy but I still had the cartoons.

HOPELESS LOVE
A VISUAL DIGRESSION FROM THE ANNALS OF SELF-ABUSE

SOMEWHERE IN THE CITY A DISEMBODIED HEAD WAS BANGING AGAINST A WALL.

NEIGHBORHOOD KIDS TEASED HEAD WHEN HE FLOATED HOME FROM WORK.

WHEN HEAD GOT BORED HE'D READ THE NEWSPAPER.

MEANWHILE, IN ANOTHER PART OF TOWN, A HEADLESS MAN NAMED ACEPHALE WAS ALSO HAVING PROBLEMS.

CONFUSED AND LONELY, ACEPHALE FOLLOWED HIS INCLINATION AND HEADED FOR A BAR.

CONTINUED →

95

96

-14-

FROM JENNIFER BLOWDRYER TO *NIGHTMARE* ON *ELM STREET, PART III*

Jennifer Blowdryer blows into Klubstitute wearing a fake leopard skin coat and glasses with thick black frames—no, that's not right. Try again.

Imagine you've come to a hospital to visit a sick friend when a nurse walks in and congratulates you on just giving birth to a two-headed pig. Surprised, huh? Your eyes widen, your mouth gapes, you want to say, "There must be some mistake," but you've been watching *Nightmare on Elm Street, Part III* and know anything is possible. After all, Freddie Krueger is the bastard child of one hundred maniacs so we expect his metaphors to be a bit mixed and overextended, right? Besides, now that he's dead, he can invade our dreams and assume any form. And he has such a sense of humor!

That's how Jennifer Blowdryer looks when she blows into Klubstitute in her fake leopard skin coat and thick black glasses—like she's ready for anything. Her bleached blond hair fans out like a team of detectives at the scene of a crime. Maybe those hairs are looking for clues? Maybe the one with split ends is Lieutenant Columbo?

It's been a hard day. The place where I've been sitting

zazen is experiencing difficulties—a possible scandal even. (Christians have heresies; Buddhists, scandals.) When I started sitting there it was a lizard paradise—a cool, dark cellar where you could just stare at the wall unmolested. Then this ex-junkie, ex-drag queen Zen priest moved in. He didn't care about Buddhist theology but he did care about people dying of AIDS, so he started bringing sick people in for us to take care of.

Now I'd never even been to a funeral before so this was a bit of an adjustment. I had to get over my sentimentality. Actually, the hardest part was just agreeing to be in the same place every Friday. The first PWA I took care of had dementia but that didn't bother me—we're all crazy under the surface—but the lack of clear rules did. I felt I was being asked to give up my whole life, that I had other things to do.

Then I started worrying about other things. How could I get a bearable job that would pay rent? Was my writing stupid and pointless? Could I stand to keep going to boring Saurian League meetings or was there another way to overcome my impulse to eat people? Was there any point to sitting zazen? Would I be "bad" if I stopped doing care-giving work?

"Just concentrate on your breath and stay mindful," my Zen teacher said. "You worry too much about some things and not enough about others."

Then a bunch of other Zen monks moved in, most of whom weren't very skilled at interpersonal relations (as "unemotional" as lizards one might say). Then my teacher got AIDS and died. In the absence of his charismatic leadership, a power struggle ensued. A PWA in the hospice wrote a fifty-page letter charging that he'd been abused. He related this to other scandals where Zen masters fucked their friends' wives, drank like fish, or chased someone with a gun after being mugged. The PWA was accused of having dementia. Charges flew back and forth.

In Zen Buddhism, life is perceived as an illusion. Death too. So I may "like" this and "hate" that which is okay so long as I realize it's all a dream. But if I don't, if I get too attached, then I obscure reality and create a big mess which is the condition of most of the world most of the time.

So what to do? One has go on trust to live at all but I don't want to naively trust anyone on a demented power trip. But who isn't? Nobody's perfect and every story has more than one side. If this sounds like that old joke about falling out of an airplane, but there's a haystack below, but it has a pitchfork in it, and so on; it is. No place to run, no place to hide. Freddie Krueger is everywhere and he has a wicked sense of humor so just watch your breath.

Jennifer Blowdryer seems to realize all this but it doesn't seem to faze her. Or maybe she's been freaked out for so long that she's totally fazed out. How many ex-punk rock singers survive at all? Anyway we're at Klubstitute to give a reading. After I torture the audience with a rapid fire, low key reading of the first two chapters of this tome, Jennifer comes on.

"I guess Steve Abbott can't help it if he's such a nice person," she begins sarcastically. Then she talks about this Louise Hays tape she got on expressing anger. She plays the tape and comments on it, sometimes just repeating some of Louise's phrases (e.g., "Let it out...unhuh."), which the audience finds hilarious.

Jennifer says she should be angry at her alcoholic ex-boyfriend but she can't seem to get up the steam for it. "You have to go back to your kindergarten personality to follow Louise Hay's instructions properly," she says. Jennifer says her problem is that she was fucked up in kindergarten too. She reminds me of Gracie Allen on downers, or that other Louise, Louise Lasser of *Mary Hartman*, who loved chatting about floor wax while grampa ran off to join the Hari Krishnas,

99

and a mass murderer went at it up the street.

(Kenneth Anger went to too much trouble preparing a magic mirror he could jump into to escape doomsday. It's easier to watch TV and wait for Freddie Krueger. Knowing Freddie, he wouldn't pull you into a fun show like *Burns and Allen* but something you hated, like *Three's Company*, or the electric shaver commercial where the guy says: "I liked it so much I bought the whole company." If anyone doubts the saurian nature of most Americans, consider how many hours they sit watching TV every day.)

After the reading, Jennifer and I trade books. She gives me two cuz she wants me to give one to Kathy Acker who is back in town and came to our reading but left early. The name of my book is *Wrecked Hearts*. The name of Jennifer's is *Where's My Wife?* Jennifer's first story is about the decline of white people into an ethnic curiosity. The last involves tooling around with a transsexual named Ginger, first at a Mamas and Papas concert in Stockton, then with various hustlers at the Tropicana in L.A. where Ed Asner's son, Matt, takes them to lunch at El Coyote, the last place Sharon Tate ate before she died.

As I peruse Jennifer's book, the most delicious boys swarm around me. I'm careful not to let my gaze linger on any of them because, pretty as they are, they remind me of the flies and larvae on decomposing carcasses in Peter Greenaway's *Zed and Two Naughts*. It's a postmodern flick where nothing much happens, yet so much happens you could go nuts trying to figure it all out. Two zoologists lose their wives in a car accident. One subsequently watches an eight-part film *The Origin of Life* endlessly while the other, his twin, watches speeded up video images of decay. Both get it on with a third woman (now one legged) who survived the car accident their wives both died in. There are also numerous references to

Vermeer, especially a lady in a red hat who does odd jobs. I appreciated the few favorable references Greenaway makes to lizards but doubt it helped overcome saurophobia as much as the cute Komodo dragon in *The Freshman,* starring Marlon Brando and Matthew Brodrick.

(Actually, the Komodo was really just a seven-foot-long Monitor lizard from Thailand. Real Komodos are twelve feet long and can eat their own weight in seventeen minutes. Thirty foot pythons and twenty-five-foot-long seawater crocodiles are also indigenous to the island. When the chief of a village in Komodo was asked about Komodo dragons by an anthropologist recently, he replied with a question of his own: did Michael Jackson have a new record out yet?)

These heady digressions made me thirsty, so I went to the bar for a drink while Lex Icon, the DJ for the evening, interrupted his tape of 50s Clairol radio commercials and earthquake news reports to play a new Pelagian single, a real foot tapper, as they say in the business.

> Don't you worry, don't you fret.
> Elvis has a room to let.
> Undamaged by original sin
> Elvis rules Pelagian.

> Art, drugs, rock n' roll.
> *Elvis Presley is no troll.*
> *So let's help Elvis work it out,*
> Sweat with Jesus, twist and shout.

> Some say Elvis got too fat,
> Acted like a big spoiled brat.
> But one thing we must not forget,
> Elvis loves his mamma yet.

The lyrics are so stupid that I can't believe this is the same group that did "Money, Sex, Born Again," but I guess that's how heresies go. They all seem exciting at first but get old fast. It's like Jennifer says, once you stop believing in "New" the rest of it crumbles, so she's going to take her atheism one step at a time. Being quaint removes the burden of being "new."

On the other hand, Michael Flanagan tells me of a Coil song I'm eager to hear about this angel with eyes all over its body for every soul in the world and when someone dies, one of the eyes closes and then the angel scoops them up in a burlap bag. Sounds like a trick a demon in *Hellraiser* might pull or maybe Freddie Krueger.

(I can see Freddie doing Hefty Bag commercials when Jonathan Winters croaks: "Here's one bag that can handle *any* mess!") What it boils down to, I guess, is that I prefer the gnostic heresies and those good old Borborite orgies. I'm just a glutton for sex and knowledge. (Of course, today we don't swallow cum or fuck without using condoms.)

Almost forty-eight hours have passed without my eating anyone. Better not press my luck. I go outside and hail a Yellow cab. The driver takes me up 16th Street past the funeral parlor, Cominsky-Roche which always reminds me of Rimski-Korsakov, the Russian composer. It's a strange world full of frivolity on one hand, and people dropping dead of starvation, murder, and AIDS on the other.

In 1970, one species perished every day; now one species perishes every hour. It's nice to have something uplifting to think about before going to sleep.

-15-

BLUE MONDAY

Monday morning at the Research Spectra again and I was feeling down; not down as in the chirpy "Down down down down down, down-da-dooby" of the Del Viking's 50s hit, "Come Go With Me," or down as in Nine Inch Nails's weird thrashing reverb in "Down in it" or The Bog's acid housey "I'll take you down," but deep *deep* down as in Charles Manson's "Garbage Dump," which supposedly so horripilated Stephen King's son when he first heard it that he was temporarily placed under psychiatric care.

Yes, I was that blue, and the morning paper didn't help. First, twenty-three-year-old K. Lemar Noid of Albany, Georgia held two Domino's Pizza employees hostage for six hours because he thought Domino's TV commercials showing a giggling red-hatted gremlim called "the Noid," who tried to chill pizzas before they could be delivered, were aimed at him.

Then the queen ant at the National Zoo in Washington, DC. was found decapitated. Worker ants tried to pull her through an opening that was too small and her head popped off leaving her thorax and abdomen dangling grotesquely from the ceiling. Experts said she may have continued to lay eggs hours or even days after the accident and that the ants would continue to care for their monarch as long as she smelled like a queen.

(Would they now hold their little ant fingers up to see which way the wind blew? Were the queen and her court three sheets to the wind when all this occurred? No more pilsner for these plastered pismires!)

As for me, I couldn't get the queen's head out of my mind. It lodged there obsessively, like the head of Marie Antoinette, or the story of William Tell for William Burroughs when he went home one day—influenced by "the ugly spirit" as he later put it—and shot his wife through the noggin, missing the apple entirely. ("I didn't know the gun was loaded," as Rosemary Cluny sang.)

I thought too of Dora Kent's head, surgically removed at the Alcor Life Extension Foundation in 1987 and placed in a jug of liquid nitrogen at -186 degrees centigrade, in hopes that it could eventually be "reanimated." Unfortunately, a coroner hadn't first proclaimed Dora "dead" (though her heart and breathing had stopped) so that, instead of winning praise for this feat of cyronic suspension, Dora's son Saul found himself charged with murder. Technical declarations were obtained from scientists such as Eric Drexler and Hans Moravec verifying that future medicine could return the dead to life although, privately, Moravec thought it preferable to download people's brains into computers. Meanwhile, law enforcement officials raided Alcor and found that Dora's head, like that of the queen ant, had disappeared.

Life/death, good/bad, fiction/reality...all the old boundaries, blasted by the trumpets of science, were crumbling. But why should this depress me, the lizard boy?

"*Dur Lex, sed lex*," I mutter to no one in particular picking up my first packet of Tell-A-Friend questionnaires for the week. I'd like to tell a friend, alright.

"How would you describe the American Dream: a) a

complete sham, b) a nightmare from the start, c) a set of fragile hopes dashed by Puritan fanaticism, French Rationalism and the greed and dishonesty of American politicians for the past two hundred years."

"So how's the Saurian League working out for you?" Maddy asks.

"Shit, you gonna start talking about *that*?" Lex interjects. "Just cuz I'm in the League don't mean I wanna hear about it all the time. Why don't you tell us more about those Borborites you were blabbing about Friday?"

"Tell ya what," I reply. "I'll tell you about a Borborite cult that surfaced in Persia recently if you tell me more about Count Lesard—is it a deal?"

Lex agreed so I began:

THE COPROPHILIAC CALIPH

This story comes from one of Squirmy's letters. He stopped off in Persia enroute to Burma, and he began this epistle evoking the sights, sounds and smells of his location: a casbah reeking of camel dung, sweaty arab boys, outdoor stalls of shish-ka-bob, and, in the distance, mullah's hollaring for the faithful.

Anyhow, Squirmy said he met a Swedish kid who claimed he'd been kidnapped by some renegade Borborites led by the notorious coprophiliac caliph known as Sultan I Wanna Sum Yung White Boys An I Wan'em Now. The Swedish kid said he was smoking kefir in a cafe one afternoon, and the next thing he knew he found himself hog tied in some back room with his jeans down around his ankles being eaten out by a creep who was apparently trying to ascertain if his "pudding" would be smooth and creamy enough for the Sultan's desert.

The Sultan, apparently, was a fastidious gourmet, an epicure of adolescent anuses from which he had identified some one hundred and fourty-three varities of feces. Moreover, he insisted that his boys be blond, and possessed of bottoms not only as round, firm, and smooth as his friend Shiek I Gotta An Insatiable Need's six hundred-year-old ivory chess pieces, but also that they be soundly spanked before being brought before him, so that their buttocks would glow with the blush of a baby's cheeks and be so sensitive to the Sultan's goatee that they'd shake and shimmie like bowls of jello.

In short, by all civilized standards this Borborite caliph (who in truth was probably a heteroclite, even according to Borborite doctrine, since he seemed to have little interest in ingesting sperm), his eunuchs, agents, and all his kingdom was reputed to be the most evil in Persia. Nouns conjugated with verbs and adjectives and adverbs did untoward things with one another at all hours of day and night. Juvenile delinquents the world over couldn't wait to visit his realm. Indeed, his palace was guarded by a once respectable vegetable garden that had long since been corrupted after being served at an orgiastic banquet for Lord Byron.

Now jaded, the vegetables—animated and given the gift of speech by means of the Sultan's magic (not unlike the farout science of Eric Drexler, Hans Moravec, and Saul Kent) which he won as part of a Satanic deal—held interminable conversations with each other to while away their boredom (boredom being the inevitable result of living a life of evil).

CARROT: Well peel my skin!
ZUCCHINI: Well paddle my squash!
CUCUMBER: Well boodle the Sultan's bunghole with a
    can of pine scented Air-wick!
ROSE OF SHARON: Well shiver my timbers and shake
    my roll, taking particular care to defoliate the Court

106

Jester's pubic region with Nare and replace his
stale jokes with a golden shower of my fragrant
petals, which have the amazing capacity to cause
narcolespy, gingivitis, and nymphomania.

Yes, in this allegedly Borborite realm the vegetables had
become so debauched that even the once discerning Venus
flytrap was now willing to ingest anything. At the same time,
everyone was so wearied by constant orgies that only one
limp burrito had the energy to dance a fandango. Finally, a
turnip gave a little cry sounding not unlike the de-activation
of a Bugatti's burglar alarm system by means of a remote
control button (although Ayatolla Mystava, one of the caliph's
advisors, put forward the opinion that it sounded more like
a baby goat getting rammed up the ass by a horny shepherd).

This was the den of iniquity Squirmy's friend was dragged
off to, and more than once, while being raped by the Sultan's
minions, the boy thought, "Oh, if I'd only stayed with Squirmy
whose neuroses were at least warm, cuddly, and familiar;
not as gross, smelly, and rapacious as those of these ignorant
camel drivers, who hardly know the difference between
humping a camel and banging a boy." And then the boy
thought, "I guess I really opened a can of worms this time,
which isn't such a smart idea when you're jumping out of
the frying pan and into the fire." And finally the boy thought,
"Fiddlesticks, Meow Mix—that's all we are at bottom. I know
my Swedish melancholy grows worse when I smoke kefir
but I can't help it, I'm addicted."

Then the Sultan thought (and one could tell he was
thinking by how his face started sweating, causing streaks
to run down his dirty cheeks and neck, and by how his thick
black mustache quivered lasciviously over his sensuous fat
lips which he began to bite):

"This new Swedish boy, if he was a couple of years
younger, I could have *peddled* instead of *paddled* his ass. I could
have patented his delicious anal produce and bottled it up like

Paul Newman's Italian Cheese Salad Dressing, thereby making myself the Great Hero and Liberator of All Nameless Downtrodden Ones Who Have Nothing But the Meager Hope of a Blond Boy's Shit to Sprinkle Over Their Couscous as They Await Martyrdom in the Coming Jihad Against the Great Satan America and Its Imperialist Running-Dog Lackies!"

And with this happy thought, the great Borborite "Pneumatic Drill," the Most High and Ruthless One, He of the Cleverest Tongue in the World, the Coprophiliac Caliph Sultan I Wanna Sum Yung White Boys An I Wan'em Now breathed his last, whereupon his swarthy, decissicated body was carried up to heaven by a host of nubile angels.

★ ★ ★ ★ ★

When I finished, I noticed that Lex's features were straining to keep from breaking into a dance.

"That's the most disgusting, stupid, unfair, *racist* story I've ever heard," he exploded.

"Well ex-*cuuuze* me," I countered, "but postmodern irony is where it's at and, whatever it is, it's *not* racism."

"If you think I'll buy that, why not sell me the Golden Gate Bridge while you're at it."

"Oh stuff it, you censorious cumquat. You're as bad as Jessie Helms."

"A cumquat am I," Lex countered. "If I had a cumcumber I'd ram it up your cloaca and clean your clock right here, you anti-arab armpit nooky."

"Boys, boys!" Maddy interrupted. "If you're going to start dishing each other, remember the Saurian League ground rules: principles before personalities and alliteration before truth. Two points per noun, one point per adjective, and remember, you have to run down your slurs in alphabetical order or you'll be disqualified. Oh yeah, all insults have to have appeared in print somewhere too. Got all that?"

Then, with no further ado, Lex and I began what historians would later call one of the Saurian League's most famous insult contests.

-16-

A FEW INSULTS FROM A TO Z

"You assimilationist assbender," I began, choosing my words carefully so as not to duplicate any imprecations and thereby lose points.

"Assimilationist assbender, huh," Lex repeated. "That's a pretty powerful appellation coming from an aquinious anus-gardener like yourself."

"Oh, so you're choosing to begin with barnyard imagery, huh? I should have expected as much from a boopic bumlicker such as yourself. And what products does your little farm specialize in, Lex, dingleberry jam?"

"Hardly, my bellicose buttered bunghole. Any crapulous coosters knock on my door and I'll send them over to you, the King of Catawamptious Clishmaclavers."

"And I'll send them right back to you, you callipygian cum-bucket!"

"Cocksucking cotswain," Lex retorted.

"Cheeky cheesetaster!"

"Well, I'm glad you recognize your betters at least, you disipiant douchbag."

"But not so loose nor drab as you, my dear epigean fastfanny."

"Better that than to be an erumpent faggot feretory like yourself, darling. Why I've heard you don't even scrape the flesh off your tired old relics."

"You should know, you first-to-be-fistfucked fleezer."
"I'd rather be that than a fartsniffing flamethrower like you."
"You flimflaming fudgepacker!"
"You cum-guzzling gazoomy!"
"Galavanting goose!"
"Giggling gunzle!"
"Half-baked hair pie!"
"Hebephrenic honeypot!"
"Hummingbird humper!"
"Hipflipping hysteric!"
"Hopheaded harridan!"
"Irrumating Idiot!"
"Ithyphallic jampacker!"
"Jumpentious keesterkisser!"
"Kootie infested quim-rimmer!"
"Lactating Lezzie!"
"Lobotomized lollygagger!"
"Maliferous mamamouchi!"
"Mimping myrmidon!"
"Nervous nelly!"
"Nidorous nurd!"
"Notorious noodle-nipple!"
"Overwrought omphalosychite!"
"Oogling octogenarian!"
"Popinating pizzle poacher!"
"Prurient putz!"
"Ramfeezled rakebelly!"

"Whoa! Hold it," Maddy interjected, rasing her beefy arms. "You missed the letter 'Q.' Rules are, if one person misses a letter, they forfeit; if you both miss, you have to start over. Since you both missed you have to start over and you can't reuse words that have already been used either."

"I didn't forget 'Q,'" Lex protested. "I had 'kootie-infested quim-rimmer,' for Chrissakes!"

"But you have to have your words in alphabetical order," Maddy explained. "Otherwise it doesn't count."

"If you wanna quit, I'll understand," I teased. "I mean, coming up with this highfalutin vocabulary must be quite a stretch for an allodorous ape like yourself."

"Not on your life, you anal-retentive Adamite," Lex retorted.

"Well you don't have to be so *asinine* about it, you Augean axilla!"

"Don't tell me how to act, you brumous bit of bumbreath."

"I won't so long as you empty your own bedpan, you bandoline-coated butt-thumper."

"Well aren't you wearing the big-girl's blouse, you bulimic buttplug!"

"Only for you, my constipated collywobble!"

"Better that than a consturpated clit-licker like yourself!"

"Cornholed catamite!"

"Better that than a cocksucking cotswain!"

"Oh you think so, huh, you dasypygal dickhead!"

"Indeed I do, you despicable dirty dildo!"

"Despiteous dingo!"

"Dilly-dallied dingus!"

"Donut-diddling dingbat!"

"Exaugurated entrement!

"Encorcellated eructator!"

"Erubescent escapade!"

"Fescinnine floozy!"

"Fairy-fingered furrowbutt!"

"Furry fumadiddle!"

"Foppish Foulfanny!"

"Flippant funnyfunnel!"

"Fuming fannyfungus!"

"Gnarly gooprick!"

"Gutterflopping gullybum!"

"Graveolent gugusse!"
"Gussied-up giftbox!"
"Gummy gutboodler!"
"Hairy hermaphrodite!"
"High hat heiny!"
"Hen-pecked hotpot!"
"Hermatomic hemorrhoid!"
"Hideous herpetic heresiarch!"
"Horny humunculus!"
"Intestine cleaning Ishmaelite!"
"Inebriated invert!"
"Itchy little incubus!"
"Jackhammered joyboy!"
"Juiced up jellybottom!"
"Kettle-of-piss!"
"K-Mart kewpie doll!"
"Lizard loving lingam!"
"Nothing wrong with lizards you leftover pail of hogslop!"
"Lollipop lollard!"
"Loose and loopy loser!"
"Marmoreal mattressback!"
"Mincing manpussy!"
"Mucid masochist!"
"Mollitious mutt!"
"Moubific mumpsimus monorchid!"
"Nasillating nannygoat!"
"Nasty necrophillac!"
"Nictitating ninny!"
"Nitpitcking nightbag!"
"Noxious-smelling nooky-nipper!"
"Nympho in nylons!"
"Obsequious onanist!"
"Olid ogre!"
"Ocellated oaf!"

"Odiferous oozing orifice!"
"Oinking obesity!"
"Prepubescent pee-pee drinker!"
"Poop-eating pervert!"
"You already called me that, you pusilanimous Pig!"
"I did not, you perfidious pederast!"
"Petulant prick!"
"Purpuraceous penis!"
"Priapic old poger!"
"Pucillating pinkpot!"
"Prurient punkhole!"
"Quonking queer!"
"Quivering quakebottom!"
"Quaint dainty-dish!"
"Querulous queen!"
"Quawking queezemadam!"
"Quidnunc Quisling!"
"Reverend Rearend Roto-Rooter!"
"Reptating rantallion!"
"Retromingent ridgeling!"
"Ructating rumpsucker!"
"Rumpfed runyon!"
"Rhumey retching runnybutt!"
"Sarcophilous sullied strumpet!"
"Scabies-infested sausage-grinder!"
"Scaturient sardoodledum!"
"Sculiferous shrew!"
"Scum-eating shill!"
"Sick sadist!"
"Slimy backdoor spermbank!"
"Slobbering slut!"
"Sloomy smellfungus!"
"Snotiformed scrump!"
"Spittal sport!"

"Spintry spunk!"

"Spumescent snollygoster!"

"Slippery squamatious sphincter!"

"Tearjerking toaster buns!"

"Tightassed tart!"

"Tedious trick!"

"Titillating tramp!"

"Afterhours trollhole!"

"Thersitical twiddlepoop!"

"Toadfucking troglodyte!"

"Transmogrified tuzziwuzzy!"

"Tunnel of fudge!"

"Tumescent-tongued twerp!"

"Turkey-necked turd-burglar!"

"Tired old twit!"

"Ubiqitous urinator!"

"Umbraceous urp!"

"Ugly unwashed—oh shit, I can't think!"

"Voluminous vat of vampire vomit!"

"Vainglorious varoshka!"

"Vellicating villain!"

"Vaccimulgent *vade mecum*!"

"Womb wallowing wombat!"

"Woozy wilted wienie washer!"

"Meet Wee Willie Wanker!"

"And his Wambling Wimp!"

"With the Wigged-out Whangdoodle!"

"Xeronic xanthrochoid!"

"Uh, uh... you xylotomous xyster!"

"You probably don't even know what that means, you yammering yahoo!"

"I do too you yellow-bellied yak puncher. It means your fucking is about as productive as sticking a surgeon's knife into a piece of wood."

"Oh shut up, you re-exumed zealot!"
"I will if you will, you cum-caked zendikite!"
"Zit-marked zebra!"
"Zymotic zygote!"
"Zoo full of Zulu zilch!"
"Zoroastrian Zorro!"
"Zendo full of..." I paused, z's buzzing through my mind like the letter repeated in comic strip snores. "Zendo full of zonked out Zippys!"

* * * * *

At this, Lex fell on the floor exhausted and I was declared the winner by a score of two hundred sixty-two to two hundred fifty-nine. I'd done it! I'd beaten the fastest chameleon tongue in the west! And to top it off, Lex now had to tell me a story of Count Lesard!

-17-

ANOTHER CHAPTER OF OUTRAGEOUS
LIES, OR
DO YOU LIVE IN A CAVE?

"So you wanna hear more about Count Lesard, huh?"

Lex paused. Having just lost the Saurian League's longest insult contest, his throat as well as his skin felt dry. Since his body, sharing a condition peculiar to both lizards and humans, was a machine adapted to making quick movements against slight resistance, and since his muscles were also enervated functionally—that is, every movement such as a joint flexion initiated by one center in the central nervous system causing all muscles concerned to contract—this dryness translated itself into "an itch" which, within less than half a second, was relayed to Lex's brain whereupon a chemical/nerve reaction commanded his right brachialis, brachioradialis, biceps brachii, and promoter teres muscles (not to mention some fifty other muscles in his wrist, hand, and fingers) to initiate a scratching motion on his neck.

It helped, but not much. So as Lex began his story, he couldn't help but think of Morrissey, in "Nov. Spawned a Monster," singing:

> a frame of useless limbs
> WHAT could make GOOD
> all the BAD that's been done?

This bit of morbidity in turn reminded Lex of Nick Cave who, in his best rebellious Jim Morrison voice, hollers, "Hands up everyone who wants to die" at the beginning of "The Bad Seed." This in turn brings Bongwater's Ann Magnusson to mind (yes, the very same who seduced River Phoenix in *The Many Loves of Jimmy Reardon*) where, on the *Power of Pussy* album, she gushes, "Wow! They have Nick Cave dolls now? I *want* one!" Which just goes to show, from Plato to rock n roll, how everything's hopelessly interconnected.

"Well, as you recall from reading *The Green Book*," Lex begins finally, "Count Lesard was blessed with powers of telepathy as well as an uncanny ability to remember the future instead of the past. But what did this mean? Did knowing the future deny or inhibit his excercise of free will? And, if so, were his ethical imperatives different from ours? I answer no to both questions for the following reasons:

First, if we take Count Lesard's words at face value— and there's no external reason not to—we must conclude that he knew the future in *all* its aspects, namely: a) what *could* be (or what grammarians call "the conditional"), b) what *will* be (or "the simple future") and c) what we'd *like* or *wish* to have be (for which there's no grammatical term but which I will call "the dream future").

Further complicating this problem is *whose* future did Count Lesard know: his own alone, his own as it intertwined with just a few others (those he ate, for instance), or did he know the future of the entire universe? Since Lesard speaks only of "remembering the future instead of the past," and since the examples he gives are fairly mundane, I would argue that he only knew the future as most of us know the past, namely as it casually intertwined with interests and people he personally interacted with.[1] Moreover, Lesard

---

[1] Lesard couldn't have "studied" the future as historians do the past since no mortal but he knew it, aside from a few speculators such as Nostradamus, Jules Verne, and H.G. Wells.

may even have forgotten some of this future as he grew older, just as many people forget bits of the past as they age. In other words, the *range* of Lesard's future awareness was no doubt as "spotty" as most people's awareness of the past. The extent of Count Lesard's free will, then, must be confined to the question of his knowledge of the future in its grammatical aspects.

"Now many of us have experienced wishes or considered what might happen if we did one thing or another (go to bed with Mr. or Mrs. X, for instance), but what would it be like if we also *knew* the third note of this chord, the future imperative? I might know that it's *possible* Mrs. X could love me and/or hope that she would, but even if I knew she would *never* really love me (or would do so for only a little while) I might *still* choose to go to bed with her or fall in love with her. Thus, even knowing that bedding Mrs. X in this instance would eventually prove inharmonious—"striking a sour chord," so to speak—it's equally possible that this dissonance between possibility, wish and eventual outcome might create an even more compelling harmony such as only Lesard's ears could imagine (i.e., think of Chaos Theory in physics: chaos lies within every system of order, but all chaos also has a deeper system of order embedded within it). In summary, since neither possibility in our paradigm can be logically or morally excluded, we must allow that Count Lesard enjoyed the same kind of ethical freedom as anyone."

"Let's see if I get this," Jim said, looking up from his Tell-a-friend Questionnaires and scratching his head. "You're saying Lesard's ethics are based on aesthetics, not morality."

"Ya, like the ancient Athenians. And I was using music as my metaphor since that's what all of us here know best."

"Okay," I interjected. "Let's see if I can illustrate what you've said with an example. Take the Beatles' song 'Dear Prudence.' The chorus—'Round and round and round and round...'—is clearly fatalistic. It's even stuck on just one note so we *know* these dudes will just *never* get off their treadmill. But

119

love, in Paul McCartney's view anyway, leaps beyond boundaries—that's its tragedy and glory—so the plaintive solo melody of the singer's desire (i.e., 'Dear Prudence, won't you come out and play-iee' with the final little torque on the word 'play') counterpoints the song's choral underpinnings just as Romeo and Juliet's balcony soliloquies do their families' tragic feud in Shakespeare's play."

"Ya, that's one way to look at it. But you could say it more simply too, like Bongwater sings:

> I don't need therapy
> I don't need religion
> I don't need new drugs
> I need a new tape.

But *needing* a new tape and getting one are two different things. See, most people are just passive consumers. If their fave band doesn't have a new tape, they'll just sit and complain. But sometimes you get someone, like Count Lesard, or John Lennon, or David Byrne, who actually does something radically new. They don't exactly know *what* they're going to do—in fact they might start off feeling totally confused and frustrated—but they persist and believe, despite all the evidence to the contrary, that they're destined for greatness.

"Do you think it's just sheer coincidence, for instance, that David Byrne started out as a goofy conceptual artist, or that his first band was called 'The Revelations,' or that he worked a summer as a Good Humor man, and then with primates (his favorite being a female named Jerome)? Do you think it was just luck that he became friends with John Waters and Edith Massy, the weirdest and most infamous people in Baltimore? Hardly! I mean it hardly even matters, since he so obviously aligned his three grammatical futures so that everything came together as The Talking Heads: his Balinese monkey chants, his big suit, his weird lyrics fusing surrealist poetry and Revivalist tent preaching, and his collaborations

120

with Brian Eno, whose "Baby's on Fire" parallelled Byrne's own "Burning Down the House." I mean Byrne/Eno virtually replaced Lennon/McCartney as the eros/thanatos twins for awhile. You can't tell me they didn't *know* this was going to happen. Hell, they planned it!

"So that's the ethics of a star—you just do it! I mean look at Madonna or Michael Jackson—and Madonna can't even sing. Still, she knows everything she does will be a smashing hit.

"Well, that's what it was like for Count Lesard. He just had this incredible intuition and, as a result, he knew that he and other later homosaurians like us would eventually tire of eating people. He did all this groovy artistic shit too, but his big contribution was founding The Saurian League and writing *The Green Book*. That's why we remember him.

"But if you really take what he says about the future seriously, the really important thing is to realize his work isn't finished yet. It's still unfolding even as we stand here talking. Like what position should we take on cryonics—freezing one's deceased body in liquid nitrogen to later be reanimated by nanotechnology? (And did you know that in Brian Yuzma's *Bride of Re-Amimator* the reanimating solution is the amniotic fluid of an iguana? Put *that* in your South Sea's pipe and smoke it!) Or take Hans Moravac, how should we view his proposal that it's possible to attain immortality by downloading your brain into a computer, a roboticized computer that could also have the consciousness of a bird or tree or god knows what added to it? Could Count Lesard, who ate some of the most talented and forward looking people of his generation, have had no inkling whatsoever of these possibilities? Hardly!"

"So what's your point, Lex? If Lesard was *fully* conscious of the future, then the future as we understand it would be dead. In fact this is already happening in art. All of art's technical achievements—the use of perspective and shading to create realistic illusions, all the various permutations of cubism, expressionism, abstractionism, and collage—all these developments have been more or less fulfilled. So all that's left

121

is theory—trying to generate new readings or interpretations of the same old territory. Or, as Nick Cave sings: 'Deep in the woods a funeral's swinging.'"

"But this historical self-consciousness is *only* a map," Lex replies. "It's *not* the territory. And there'll always be enough variance between map and territory that we can create free autonomous zones, cracks or folds where we can act and generate new meaning. So artists, scientists, and computer hackers will be our new pioneers, our pirates of the future.

"So 'my point,' as you put it, is this: I don't think Count Lesard intended for *The Green Book* to become a bible or his Saurian League to become a church. That would totally violate everything he stood for. He intended for us to keep moving, changing, evolving, and growing.

"If Count Lesard could be reanimated today, instead of taking on the body of an obscure artist such as Odilon Redon again, I think he'd choose to make horror flicks like David Cronenburg or Wes Craven. Or maybe he'd leapfrog all that pretentious shit and opt to front a band like FEEDERZ, whose vocalist, Frank Discussion, glued live crickets to his head when they last played Gilman Street. Ya, or he'd choose to edit some queer 'zine like *Thing, Bimbox, Diseased Pariah News,* or *The Fertile Latoyah Jackson Newsletter* or whatever. And maybe *that's* how he'd get his ideas out today.

"So what we gotta do is stop puzzling over the aphorisms Lesard wrote one hundred years ago, and start networking with other homosaurians around the world to figure out why there's this big fear of a Lizard Planet. I mean we lizards didn't pollute this earth. We're not threatening its survival. So why must we keep hiding our tails between our legs and apologizing for our existence? As far as I'm concerned, we've got no reason to hide in caves anymore, regardless of whether they're Platonic, Nickian, or whatever. So the only questions left are: a) does Lesard really want to stick his tongue up our metaphorical asses from the grave? and b) if he does, can we stand the liberating estasy of finding out exactly what this heretical Borborite gnostic ass kissing might be like?"

122

-18-

A FINAL DESPERATE STAB AT ENLARGING
THIS NOVEL'S UNIVERSE

Iconic Lex was impossible when he got to philosophizing, but I understood what he meant. Now that I'd stopped eating people, I had to decide what to do with my life. It was no freedom to escape the conformity of mainstream culture only to adhere even more rigidly to some counterculture's dogmas (e.g., getting tatoos, wearing chains and black leather, wearing baseball caps backwards, etc.).

So in a final desperate attempt at enlarging this novel's universe I employed my market research skills and devised several questionnaires, which I mailed out in the summer of 1991 to some 60 'zine editors, artists, musicians, writers, and friends around the USA and elsewhere. Twenty-five responses were returned, five of which were from women. As for a geographical breakdown, five responses came from outside the U.S.A., six came from the NYC/East Coast area, seven from the Midwest, and seven from the West Coast. In terms of occupational categories there was some overlap, but nine respondents were writers (poets, novelists or journalists), eight were editors, four were students, three musicians, and one was an artist.

[NOTE: IN CASE YOU HAVEN'T NOTICED, THIS ISN'T A "REAL NOVEL" ANYWAY. IT'S AN ANARCHIST HANDBOOK OF GUERRILA WARFARE TACTICS.]

Complicating my survey compilation, however, was the fact that I varied the wording on different questionnaires and couldn't recall which ones I'd sent to which people. Moreover, one respondent "cut-up" his answers, so I had to fit them together as best I could. Four respondents, associated with the 'zine *Virus 23* in Canada, answered their questions on an overnight roadtrip to see Jimmy Swaggart preach. Not everyone answered all the questions. The following includes verbatim answers to each question as well as some percentage breakdowns.

QUESTIONNAIRE

1) What are Your Favorite Music Groups and Why? (Quote Some Lyrics)

> **The Smiths'** lyrics strongly influenced my youth to age twenty-two ("I wear it black on the outside `cuz black is how I feel on the inside."). Now I like **The Pixies** more.
> —Theo Monnier, Paris, FRANCE.
> (journalist)
>
> "Fuck the Dead. Fuck the Dead. Fuck the Dead." **Gwar**; "I'm bud the spud from the gread red mud just rollin' down the highway smiling" **Stompin Tom Connors**; "I saw an X-ray of a girl passing gas." **Butthole Surfers**; "Don't you ever just want to kill the stupid people?" *Boyd Rice*.
> —Bruce Fletcher, J. G., J., Pransky, and Eric Fletcher respectively, of *Virus 23*, Red Deer, Alberta CANADA.

124

I refuse to commit myself to idolatry in print—at least more than I've already done in other interviews which invariably and horribly misquoted me.

— Diamanda Galas, NYC.
(Shriek opera diva)

The Beatles (esp. John Lennon who revolutionized rock lyrics).

—Steven Taylor, NYC.
(musician/singer)

Don't have any favorite groups. Maybe **The Sons of the Pioneers** ("All day I face/ The barren waste/ Without the taste/ Of water/ Cool water.").

— Alice Notley, poet, NYC.
(co-editor of *Scarlet*)

The King Farouk Memorial Orchestra, playing nitely at Hotel Palais Des Vents, Alexandria, 1911.

— Hakim Bey, NYC.
(anarchist theoretician)

Fishbone, Red Hot Chili Peppers, Miles Davis, Charlie Parker, Wagner, Vivaldi.

— Russell Goodman, E. Northpoint, NY.
(student)

When I was younger (not that long ago) I adored **The Smiths, The Eurythmics**, and **Kiss**. Mom took me to see **Kiss** in concert in 79, a great show with lots of explosions and fire. Gene spit blood and Ace broke his guitar. I loved it. It was the first concert I ever saw. The first two records I ever bought were **K-Tel**'s *Disco Rocket* and **The Sugarhill Gang**'s *Rapper's Delight*.

My fave song right now is "Gypsy Woman (she's homeless)" by Baltimore's **Crystal Waters** produced by the Basement Boys. Also, when I saw **Diamanda Galas** perform "Have you seen the face of the devil" I started crying and couldn't stop. It was the closest thing to a spiritual experience I've ever had.

— Seth S., Washington, D.C.
(student)

De La Soul, Can, John Coltrane Quartet, Sonic Youth, Pere Ubu, Ntynem, Jungle Brothers, Shangri-Las, old Kinks, Fifth Column, Joy Division, Jimi Hendrix Experience, Orb, The Band of Holy Joy, My Bloody Valentine, "tons of Detroit and Chicago house groups" among others; Among lyrics quoted: "Every lightbulb's waiting" (NY Dolls), "Etcetera, etcetera, etcetera" (Smiths), "We make feasties of the beasties, but the beasties just live in the wild" (T. Rex), "Her hustler boyfriend was killed on his Ninja motorcycle in Van Nuys Califorinia USA" (Pedro Muriel y Esther).

— Steve Lafreniere, Chicago.
(writes for *Thing*, *Bimbox*)

Coil, Buzzcocks, Crass, Marc Almond, Astor Piazzolla, Live Skull, Ornette Coleman, Dave Howard Singers, Husker Du, Funkadelic and others; lyrics quoted from Coil's "Ostia (the death of Passolini)" and from "This is the day" by The The.

— Mark Freitas, Ann Arbor, MI.
(edits *PC Casualties*)

Used to like Swans whose lyrics are ultra-depressing and masochistic ("Money is flesh/ Money, flesh in your hands... When you pay, you're a servant, you deserve it..."); The Cocteau Twins—somewhat a guilty pleasure, so fey and Euro; currently I like hiphop—Consolidated, Dream Warriors, Tribe Called Quest. I like dense sound, modest rappers, unusual samples, political content, conversational delivery.

— Lawrence Roberts, MPLS, MN.
(edits *Holy Titclamps*)

Layabouts, "Fuckalot" ("You've got to dance a lot/ if you want to stay alive/ You've got to dance a lot/ if the world is to survive..."); King Missile (goofy performance poetry with post-psychedelic music).

— Sunfrog, Detroit, MI.
(edits *Babyfish*)

126

Frank Allison and **The Odd Sox** ("I know this girl who has this mental thing/ She wants everything and everything's community"); **Only a Mother** (yodels and animal sounds).

> — Lisa Last, Detroit, MI.
> (student)

Bob Dylan ("I wish just one day you could stand in my shoes so you could see what a drag it is to see you")

> — Melissa Parson, Kent, OH.
> (student)

Laurie Anderson ("The sun comes up like a big bald head"); **Concrete Blond** ("She says she was a Queen of LA/ She might have been, who am I to say?"); **Public Enemy** ("Wash your butt, honey"); **Stranglers** (for their heartfelt angst-ridden glances and their strip-tease stage acts).

> — Lorelei Berndt, Kennewi, WA.
> (student)

The Beach Boys, "In My Room"; **The Velvet Underground**, "I'll Be Your Mirror."

> — Kevin Killian, SF, CA.
> (novelist/playwright)

New York Dolls ("What do you call your lover boy? Trash!"); **The Cramps** (because all their songs have to do with trash).

> — Jerome Caja, SF, CA.
> (artist/performer)

The Eurythmics, Julia Fordham, every bitter love song written by a female, **Dead Can Dance**, **Cocteau Twins**, **This Mortal Coil**.

> — Rachel Pepper, SF, CA.
> (journalist, editor of *Cunt*)

I like the **Pet Shop Boys** for their dry humor.

> — Michael Marriner, SF, CA.
> (editor of *Xcess*)

Current faves: **Fugazi**, **Ride**, **My Bloody Valentine**; All time faves: **Velvet Underground**, **Joy Division**, **Husker Du**, **Sex Pistols**, **Sonic Youth**, **Jesus and Mary Chain** (only *Psychocandy* album), **Echo and the Bunnymen** (only *Heaven Up Here* album) **Cheap Trick**, **The Smiths**,

127

Butthole Surfers (in concert only). I like these groups for their seduction (melody, hook), lyrics (language curiously underhoned to be filled out by music and vocal intonation) and experiments in the musicianship which I find particularly useful in studies re. my writing.

— Dennis Cooper, LA, CA.
(novelist)

Dinosaur Jr. ("So don't let me fuck up will you, 'cause when I need a friend it's still you."); **Ride, Lush** ("What's *that* supposed to mean?"), **Sonic Youth, Public Enemy, My Bloody Valentine**.

— Mark Ewert, LA, CA.
(writer)

2) Do you believe in UFOs? If so, how much?

A. Percentage breakdown

YES 8
NO 6
BELIEVE LIFE
ELSEWHERE IN
UNIVERSE 2
OTHER 2
DON'T KNOW 2
NO ANSWER 5

B. Verbatim answers:

I don't believe UFOs fly over deserted highways, but I am convinced that somewhere in the universe (do I sound like Carl Sagan?) there is life similar to ours.

— Theo Monnier.

Enough to believe aliens visit us.

—J.P.

Yes, it would be stupid not to because so many people see it as reality, therefore they do exist. Besides, UFOs are anything that's undentified.

— Eric Fletcher.

128

It depends on who I am that day.

No.

— Diamanda Galas.

Yes, but *what* are they—hallucinations, projections of mandala, or what?

— Steven Taylor.

Not especially. I usually feel impatient with people who say they've seen one.

— Alice Notley.

Best hypothesis on UFOs: They're forms taken nowadays by the *djinn*, beings created of fire which are neither real nor unreal but imaginal who can get into everybody's dreams. They're also capable of being controlled by magicians of sufficient power.

— Hakim Bey.

I believe in UFOs very much because I don't think we can be the only intelligent beings in the universe.

— Russell Goodman, NY.

I believe in UFOs because I saw one when I was fifteen. It was a traumatic event as I was undergoing psychiatric treatment at the time for temporary psychosis, too many pschedelics ingested. I was an outpatient and was in the mountains outside Denver with a high school friend who saw it too. A very large, dark shape passed slowly over the sky about three hundred feet up, not unlike some of the scenes in *Close Encounters*. Completely evil and creepy. It went behind the mountain.

— Steve Lafreniere.

I probably don't, but I do collect 50s UFO hysteria.

— Mark Freitas.

No, stars are too far away and I don't believe earth-made UFOs were a possibility in the 50s.

— Lawrence Roberts.

Yes, I believe in everything.

— Sunfrog.

My father, who's an astronomer, says that in all his years of observing he's never seen anything he

129

couldn't identify. Neither have I.

— Lorelei Berndt.

Yes. (see extensive verbatim answer, next chapter)

— Kevin Killian.

No, not until I get a ride.

— Jerome Caja.

I believe in the possibility of UFOs. I'd hate to think that we're the best that's evolved in the universe.

— Rachel Pepper, SF.

I believe in UFOs a little, wanting it to be true, figuring odds are...

— Dennis Cooper.

I believe in astrology, astral gates, kabbala, tarot, ESP, Ouiji Boards, Divination, prophetic dreams, ghosts, PSI phenomenon, curses, and Voodoo—cuz it's interesting to think about. For some reason UFOs always left me *icy,* so I was never interested enough to believe in them.

— Mark Ewert.

Not only do I believe in UFOs, I believe earth was colonized by spirits from outer space. But we've forgotten why we came here, which is why UFOs return—to remind us.

— X2000, Austin, TX.
(musician)

3) What have you done that you're most ashamed of? (Don't answer this question truthfully. Make up a lie.)

Answers ranged from cheating on lovers and not putting money in charity boxes at 7-11 Stores (cuz "everyone sees you don't give") to narcing on friends and hurting animals or children. Social evils such as racism, ageism, and nuclear proliferation were also mentioned. One respondent was most ashamed of his pick-up truck. I decided to keep these answers confidential.

4) What is the nature of variations between the true and fictional answers to the above question?

Makes no sense without the answers for question 3.

5) What is the most important question for you at present?

A. Percentage breakdown:

PERSONAL 7
POLITICAL 4
PHILOSOPHICAL/
SPIRITUAL 3
OTHER 1
NO ANSWER 9

B. Verbatim answers:

Did I feed the cat?

— Eric Fletcher.

Wondering how many years do I have left so I can decide how much time I have to relax and do absolutely nothing.

— Diamanda Galas.

How to save the universe through music.

— Steven Taylor.

What to write next. This includes ramifications as to how I can stand to keep living in this city, in this country, etc.

— Alice Notley.

What am I doing with my life?

— Russell Goodman.

What makes sex "sex"?

— Mark Freitas.

What a 4th dimensional pizza would look like. Also, if all particles in the universe follow the laws of physics, is everything predestined (our brains are made of particles, so do we have free will?) Reality's a train you can't derail.

— Lawrence Roberts.

How to be my own editor/publisher and never have to work a "real" job.

— Sunfrog.

131

How can I get people to WAKE UP? How much to compromise to get into a position to affect people, if at all.

—Lorelei Berndt.

How to pay the rent.

— Kevin Killian.

What to wear to the Castro Street Fair.

— Jerome Caja.

When will I ever be able to a) get married, b) be happy being married?

— Rachel Pepper.

Why not?

— Michael Marriner.

What do I want from them?

— Mark Ewert.

Why are you asking all these questions? How do I know you're not with the CIA?

—X2000.

6) What are one or two of your favorite sentences?

"Nothing is true; everything is permitted."; "Hey buddy, you got a dead cat in there?" (Bruce Fletcher); "Get your ass to mass."; "Sorry officer, I didn't mean to." (Eric Fletcher); "They'll never notice it's missing." (J.G.)

— *Virus 23* group.

"I love you. I really do, you know."; "Thank you."

— Steven Taylor.

"Mrs. Ringer was born interested." (Willa Cather, *Sapphira and the Slave Girl*); "No white shall ever see the tears of a Menominee." (Robert Anton Wilson, *Illuminatus Trilogy*).

— Alice Notley, NYC

Animals were condemned to punishment in the middle ages. The proposed Massachusetts law making it illegal to draw or paint underage models.

— Hakim Bey.

"Nothing is good or bad but thinking makes it so." (Shakespeare)

— Russell Goodman.

When I was a TA for a creative writing class, one sentence I couldn't stop laughing about was "He strode across the floor with the fluidity of a giraffe."

— Seth S.

"If you go with this woman, within forty-seven hours you will be dead!" (The Goddess Bunny in John Aes-Nihil's remake of *The Roman Spring of Mrs. Stone*); "Which would you prefer, a wedding or a funeral out at sea?" (Mabel in Ronald Firbank's *Inclinations*).

— Steve Lafreniere.

Rimbaud's "Visionary" letter and the section of Raymond Radiquet's *Devil in the Flesh* where he talks about looking for one's image in all you see.

— Mark Freitas.

"I'm like, why?"; "She's fun as shit and cool as hell."

— Lawrence Roberts.

Ten years hard labor writing poetry under a mango tree.

— Sunfrog.

"Bug off, dickface."; "The more you know, the less you understand."

— Melissa Parson.

"Go to the store, go to the store, go to the store and then die." (Alice Notley)

— Lorelei Berndt.

"A man may sail so at sea, as that he shall have laid the north pole flat, that shall be fallen out of sight, and yet he shall not have raised that south pole, he shall not see that; so there are things in which a man may go beyond his reason, and yet not meet with faith neither." (John Donne, *Sermon LXXVI*, II, 385)

— Kevin Killian.

"I'm lookin' for some trouble" and "I'm gonna kick your ass." (Those are the two sentences I use most.)

— Jerome Caja.

"She shrieked in horror."; "You bitch!"

— Rachel Pepper.

The more things change, the more they stay the same;
Dollars for donuts.

— Michael Marriner.

"When you're expecting bad news you have to be
prepared for it a long time ahead so that when the
telegram comes you can already pronounce the
syllables in your mouth before opening it." (Robert
Pinget); "Put all the images in language in a place of
safety and make use of them, for they are in the desert,
and it's in the desert we must go and look for them."
(Jean Genet)

— Dennis Cooper.

Last line of *Lord of the Rings*: "'Well, I'm home,' he said."

— Mark Ewert.

"What you mean 'we,' white man?" (Tonto to Lone
Ranger in *Mad* magazine); "Do you want to know me or
kiss me?" (Fassbinder's *Lola*)

—X2000.

7) What are your favorite movies, and why?

The Ten Commandments by the Polish director Kieslowsky
because of its sensuosity, its use of religious symbols, its
asking questions without giving answers. I also like Woody
Allen's and Rohmer's movies, *Blade Runner*, and Monty
Python's *Holy Grail*.

— Theo Monnier.

*A Clockwork Orange, Videodrome, The Cook, the Thief, his
Wife and her Lover* (J.P.); *Bladerunner, The War, Withnail and
I* (J.G.); *20,000 Leagues Under the Sea, Planet of the Apes*
(because of Charlton Heston), *Aerobisex Girls, White of the
Eye, The Blob* (all versions) and all handmade films (Eric
Fletcher); *Don't Look Now, Dead Ringers, Dawn of the Dead*
& vampire movies (Bruce Fletcher)

— *Virus 23* group.

I suppose people would expect me to say *Salo* or *El Topo* but I prefer any film with Doris Day. She makes me feel so clean. Also Robert Taylor films.

— Diamanda Galas.

Hamlet ('41 version), *Rules of the Game*, *The Searchers*, *She Wore a Yellow Ribbon*, *Ninotchka*, the Star Wars movies. They're all movies I could see over and over. I'm facinated by John Ford's use of a social group as the real hero— includes people of different ages, comic figures, various ethnic groups, etc. I also like the respectful distance (camera-wise) Ford keeps from the characters.

— Alice Notley.

P as in Pelican, an Iranian film about a boy and a pelican who mysteriously lived in the middle of a desert town called Tabas (later destroyed in a 1978 earthquake); *Wild Blackberries*, a French short about boys who play naked Indians and pirates in the woods; *Godzilla vs. the Smog Monster*, best agitprop ever except for *Do Dialectics Break Bricks?*, a re-dubbed Kung Fu flick.

— Hakim Bey.

Dune by David Lynch (every expectation is aggravated and every character betrays themself); *The Golden Eighties* and *The Eighties* by Chantal Ackerman (the former, the videotaped auditions for the latter. Like Jack Smith, Ackerman has evidently bribed the timing gods); *Evil Dead 2* by Sam Raimi (exactly like a relentless, funny nightmare); *The Color of Pomegranates* by Sergei Parajanov (also like a funny nightmare but calmer than *Evil Dead 2*); *The Black Lizard* by some 60s Japanese filmmaker (from opening shots of dayglo Beardsley wallpaper at discoteque to the gallery of living statues that includes Mishima, this is one of the WILDEST things I've ever seen on screen); *The Doctor's Dream* by Ken Jacobs (sentimental short from the 30s rearranged scene by scene. I saw some of Jacobs' Museum of the Moving Image restrospective in NY in 89. Ken used two projectors and a homemade stobe effect allowing

only one projector's image to be seen at a time. The
film was the earliest known celluloid porn; *Ciao Manhattan*
by Paul Morrissey. (I saw this in 74 in Denver and it
had a profound effect on me, esp. on my fashion sense.)

— Steve Lafreniere.

Kenneth Anger films (for their queerness and use of
magick); Kubrick, Gus Van Sant and early Almodovar
films; also Genet's *Un Chant D'Amour,* and *Pump Up the
Volume*.

— Mark Freitas.

A Stan Brakhage movie that tries to imitate what you
see when your eyes are closed, *The Many Adventures of
Winnie the Pooh, Horizons in the Midst*.

— Lisa Last.

Vampire movies from Hong Kong (*Chinese Ghost Story,
Zu Warriors of the Magic Mountain,* etc.). Also Jackie
Chan's *Police Story 2*.

— Lawrence Roberts,.

Do The Right Thing; Eating (Because it shows we ladies
have a long road ahead to plow away bogus ideals for
fashionable bodies).

— Melissa Parson.

Wim Wenders' *Wings of Desire*.

— Lorelei Brendt.

*West Side Story, Valley of the Dolls, Flower Drum Song,
Finian's Rainbow, Viva Las Vegas* (because of their *joie de
vivre* and youth consciousness).

— Kevin Killian.

Aliens, cuz Signorey is so hot. Also *Paris Is Burning*.

— Rachel Pepper.

Fellini's *Juliet of the Spirits* for its light, airy feeling;
Kubrick's *2001,* because it created something better
than I could imagine.

— Michael Marriner.

Bresson's *The Devil Probably, Four Nights of a Dreamer,*
and *Lancelot du Lac,* Warhol's *Chelsea Girls,* Anger's
Inauguration of the Pleasure Dome, Welle's *The Magnificent
Ambersons,* Ozu's *Late Spring,* Hunter's *River's Edge,*

Fellini's *Satyricon*, Renais' *Providence*, Bertolucci's *Luna*.
All shaped me and maintain power after many
viewings.

— Dennis Cooper.

Relaxing movies like *Logan's Run* or *Planet of the Apes*.
I also like dorky fantasy films like *Labyrinth*, *Legend*,
The Dark Crystal, *Beastmaster*. *The Wizard of Oz* is my
idea of the totally perfect movie.

— Mark Ewert.

8) If you could download your brain into a computer, would you
do so? Would this make you eternal?

8A. Percentage breakdown:

YES	6
YES, WITH QUALIFICATION	2
NO	7
NO, WITH QUALIFICATION	3
NO ANSWER	7

8B. Would it make you eternal?

YES	2
NO	2
WHAT'S ETERNITY?	2
DON'T KNOW	1
NO ANSWER	18

Verbatim answers:

I wouldn't care to have my mind downloaded into a
computer although it might be interesting if I could
return to a body after a few centuries. But I'd probably
have the same problems: to find a real love, make
money, have an interesting job.

— Theo Monnier.

137

Maybe, if I got a horrendous terminal disease when I was young, but otherwise no. I like flesh and how would I understand death if I was downloaded? But it probably would be an interesting simulacrum if you lived in virtual reality.

— Bruce Fletcher.

No, I wouldn't want to be someone's info directory. And it wouldn't make you eternal—nothing's eternal. I'd much rather be downloaded into something or someone organic.

— Eric Fletcher.

Unfortunately I'm not under the illusion that my mind would be that amusing to save.

— Diamanda Galas.

Yes, if I could then play with it. Eternity, what's that?

— Steven Taylor.

Yes, because I'd like this type of information to be available. At the same time something like that could easily turn into another oppressive institution. Who'd be included? Would minds be "edited" or "cataloged"? (If I wasn't in charge of how my mind was presented, it wouldn't be "mine".) What would it cost? Would "mind terminals" be available everywhere or would only some people's minds be available in some places? I'd like to see history move beyond the thoughts and lives of an elite and to see how my own thoughts might correlate with everyone's, but I'd mainly be concerned with who, how, by whom, for whom, etc.

— Seth S.

I guess so. We're all eternal anyway, right?

— Steve Lafreniere.

I'm not interested in living longer; I want to live "wider" (to quote Jimi Hendrix). I'd like to operate my word processor by just thinking, not typing or talking, (so that) the computer becomes part of you like a hand. An entire person on a computer would be like a play on TV, similar but the wrong media. I think there's something about our bodies we can't do without and still be who we are. (If your brain was on a computer, could you still do LSD?)

— Mark Freitas.

The flesh becomes floppy disk? Can't get with that.

— Sunfrog.

Yes, I'd do it because I have some valuable insights....It wouldn't make me eternal.

— Melissa Parson.

Download—yes, but only if it could be done without destroying the original. If I was dead I'd do it. You could have lots of copies and one might be eternal. They'd get warped like multi-generation tape dubs. But if I could be eternal, would I ever create anything, immortality being one reason mortals create.

— Lawrence Roberts.

It would depend on how thorough the download was (conscious *and* unconscious mind?). No, you'd need my unique facial expressions and vocal tones.

— Lorelei Brendt.

My mind downloaded into a computer—like HAL in *2001*? Sure, that would make me immortal.

— Kevin Killian.

Seems like an awful waste. Besides, it would make lying so difficult.

— Jerome Caja.

It would only make you eternal until someone erased it, but I think I might do it. It would be interesting to see just how brilliant I could get.

— Rachel Pepper.

No.

— Michael Marriner.

It would have to be a pretty good machine to accept a person's complete mind but I guess I would, which surprises me cuz I like the idea of getting old and then dying.

— Mark Ewert.

Shit no! People are too much like machines already, just doing what they've been programed to do.

—X2000.

9) How do you feel about lizards? Do you think it would be possible for someone to be a "Homosaurian", or not? And, if so, should they join a Saurian Recovery League?

Percentage breakdown:

9A. How feel about lizards?

LIKE	8
DISLIKE	2
NEUTRAL	3
OTHER	5
NO ANSWER	7

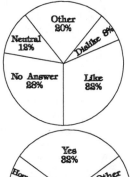

9B. Possible to be Homosaurian?

YES	8
NO	0
WHAT'S A HOMOSAURIAN	2
OTHER	2
NO ANSWER	13

Verbatim answers:

I like lizards okay. "Homosaurians" reminds me of the TV serial *V*.

— Theo Monnier.

Anything is possible, especially homosaurians. Just watch a *Startrek* episode, lots of their aliens are reptiles. I don't know if they should join a Saurian Recovery League. Maybe Fundamentalist Saurianism would be better.

— Eric Fletcher.

I think it's possible to be homosaurian, although I feel my particular ancestry is more related to arachnids.

— Diamanda Galas.

I like lizards.

— Steven Taylor.

I like lizards. I used to catch them when I was a kid (in Arizona). I find as an adult though that I can't touch those beautiful creepy big ones that the punks like to carry around. I don't know what "homosaurian" means.

— Alice Notley.

Fuck those New Age pundits who badmouth the reptilian brain! At the reptile house in the zoo I peer through opera-glasses at the jewelled hieroglyphs of lizards' skins like a Taoist medium scrying the tadpole script of mysterious spirit texts. Outside, an August rain falls in sheets of greygreen the way Castaneda said would open a curtain on the Other World, soft and shivering.

Young boys love the reptile house, like a red haired twelve-year-old who's materialized next to me out of the Linnean darkness. Topaz eyes, pale skin. Corelli's music filters through the foul smelling air, music transparent as amber reptiles sunning themselves on the wet, silvery stones of Venice. Mesmerized by the lizards' gaze behind the glass, the boy's hand slips into his pants emerging fondling a stiff, legless lizard white as a mushroom tipped in pink. He bites my neck and shoots dribs of moonslime on the protective glass. Ah, how the iguanas, those four-legged emerald cocks, would love to tongue up that pollen. Now I'm holding him up as he gasps for breath collapsed against me. With a little UFO giggle, he pisses. Warm urine splatters thru my fingers and against the glass as the lizards leap away expecting to be drenched.

A chorus of frogs in derby hats cheers our insouci-ance. Loll back and lick a cane-toad. This is the heretical doctrine of the Starry Wisdom Sect of boy-worshipping pseudo-dervishes, Haschhisch cults of Hidden Hoodoo Masters of the Dismal Swamp. Tadpole Scriptures on the walls of flowerchoked latrines. Snakeskin cockring jackoff Gospel to the Reptilians. Libertine Orphites licking silver dishes of pubescent semen. *Hoc est jism meum*. Saltsweet hairless armpits of the Naughty Child God. Dragon rafters cloaked in soddenswirling Twin Rabbit Mosquito Coil Incense..... Nipple rings, dragon tattoos. And the redhaired boy tying a cat's-cradle diamond pattern like a reptile's back....

Gimmie that ole time Mesozoic religion, little salty dick on my tongue, backbrain, crackbrain homosaurian prophet boys of the August rain!

— Hakim Bey.

I guess lizards are okay. I haven't really hung out with that many.

— Russell Goodman.

Lizards are lowly creatures and way overused these days, iconically speaking.

— Steve Lafreniere.

Most boys of my generation grew up on dinosaur mania (dragons are another kid fantasy). Lizards are the closest thing in the "real" world. Also, I was facinated by the Galapagos Island Iguanas in bezillions of PBS documentaries I saw as a kid. Now I like the smaller lizards—geckos and true chameleons.

— Mark Freitas.

I like licking, listening to and seeing lizards. Homosaurians are fully probable since you can already be part human and part cop.

— Sunfrog.

When a human's skin is hot, it's like a fever; when a lizard's is hot, it's like a sun warmed stone. Have you ever eaten fresh-picked fruit on a hot day? It's made sweeter by the sun. "Cold-blooded" is a cruel term. Lizards have the same temperature as their surroundings.

It's hard to read a lizard's eyes. You could find it sexy but you wouldn't know what he thought about you. So I'd be careful about a homosaurian's intentions.

— Lawrence Roberts.

Lizards are beautiful. I'd like one to crawl over my back all night to comfort me. I think it's possible someone could be homosaurian.

— Melissa Parson.

When I was a little boy, my uncle who was a scientist kept a Komodo dragon in a room in the back of his house. He and his wife had wanted a kid and had this nursery built. The lizard was my cousin, so to speak. A horrible, ugly, scary monster big as I was. It was my alter ego—everything I felt about myself that I was too shy to admit or talk about.

— Kevin Killian.

I love lizards because they're so pretty. I don't know if if I've met any lizard people or not but I've met some who are pretty clammy. One guy I was makin' out with was called "the lizard man" cuz he had bad skin.

— Jerome Caja.

Lizards make good pets but I think it's cruel to keep them.

— Rachel Pepper.

I don't feel kindly toward lizards. What does homosaurian mean? Attracted to lizards or half-human, half-lizard?

— Michael Marriner.

Don't have feelings one way or the other about lizards. Anyone can be anything and fuck recovery groups.

— Dennis Cooper.

I always thought it would be cool to have a lizard but would probably be happy when it died. I've killed *all* of my pets. As for a homosaurian, ya, I think it's possible but only if the person turned into a regular, small sized lizard. Movies where people go half and half or change gradually are so murky and yucky cuz the special effects are so bad. If Gregor Samsa hadn't totally transformed into a bug it would have been a stupid story.

— Mark Ewert.

I used to freak girls out by swallowing live gold fish. I don't know if that makes me like a lizard or not but once, I remember thinking it would be really rad if I could crawl on ceilings cuz then I could piss on people like a Gecko. Geckos piss from their pores and it burns if it lands on you.

—X2000.

10) What is your favorite heresy, and why?

A. Percentage breakdown:

CHRISTIAN ....*6 TOTAL*
ARIAN 1
BOGOMILE 1
CATHAR 5
CATHOLIC 1
GNOSTIC 1
MANICHEAN 1
MONIST 5
BUDDHIST 1
ISLAMIC 1
MAGIC............................. 2
NON-RELIGIOUS/
SHOCK MORAL
BELIEFS 3
OTHER 3
DON'T KNOW 1
NO ANSWER 8

B. Verbatim answers:

My fave heresy is the belief in coincidental magic
because it works so well.

— Eric Fletcher.

Cathars and gnostics who believed you shouldn't procre-
ate, though for me it was a more intuitive decision from
about the age of eight.

— Diamanda Galas.

The Arian heresy—people praying with their arms
outstretched and their palms exposed rather than with
their hands together. Hands are sexy!

— Steven Taylor.

I like the anti-work-ethic heresy. I think work sucks and
the world would be a better place if fewer people had
jobs.

—Alice Notley.

144

The Islamic heretics: Mansur ibn al-Hallaj, who was martyred for boasting "I am the Real" and writing a defense of Satan as "the perfect sufi and lover"; the Nizari Ismailis Hasan II, great grandson of the legendary Hasan-i Sabbah, who proclaimed the Qiyamat or Great Resurrection which advocated the shedding of all opinion, habit, and order; Ahmad Ghazzali and Awhadoddin Kermani who advocated the imaginal yoga of "sacred pedophilia." Add to these the Lawless Qalandar dervishs, or the Nematollahi dervishes who congregated with Hindu saddhus of the lingayat sect (phallus worshippers), and you've got a pretty wild bunch, much more dionysian than most Christian heretics.

— Hakim Bey.

My favorite heresy is that God doesn't exist because all others flow from that. I supported NAMBLA too.

— Steve Lafreniere.

Even though I liked the gnostics, I'm a hopeless monist—matter/spirit are all the same to me.

— Mark Freitas.

I like all heresies.

— Sunfrog.

My favorite Hershey is Special Dark cuz it tastes rich and leaves me feeling ill. Oh, *heresy*! Do you think communism is failing because of Fatima? (That's where the Virgin Mary appeared and said masses should be said worldwide for the end of communism.)

— Lawrence Roberts.

My favorite is probably the one that says good and evil war through the worlds—Manichean is it?

— Kevin Killian.

The Catholic Church—you can't get any more heretical than that. Most saints were heretics at one time, or else they fought some heresy or other. Of course most Catholics have no idea what their faith's about.

— Jerome Caja.

145

My favorite heresy is the picture in *Homocore* of the little boy giving head to Jesus. Also the band called **The Heretics** from Toronto.

— Rachel Pepper.

That anyone can be a good writer. Or to write well, you must have something to say.

— Michael Marriner.

I like the Bogomiles cuz they killed priests.

— Mike Flanagan, SF
(AIDS rersearcher)

Can't read your handwriting here.

— Dennis Cooper.

The only buddhist heresy would be to count on anything supernatural or outside your immediate world to save you.

— Mark Ewert.

Heresies, you mean like the Temple ov Psychic Youth? I don't know much about them except I heard they use Aleister Crowley's and William Burroughs' ideas. I dunno, they still seem kinda uptight to me.

—X2000.

-19-

KEVIN'S CHAPTER

In September, 1988, I wrote to Whitley Strieber, the horror writer whose latest books detail his thesis that ordinary Americans, men and women like ourselves, have been the victims of sex experiments by alien creatures in UFOs.

After receiving my letter, Strieber wrote back consolingly, advising me of a support group for people in my area suffering from my problem. I learned one lesson from this exchange, there's help for everybody. As Joe Orton said, "Nature excuses no one the freaks' roll call." Here's my original letter:

Dear Mr. Strieber:

Twelve years ago, I was 23, a waiter in the North Shore town of Smithtown, Long Island. I'd been visiting my parents on my way to work, and as I drove away from their house a startling thing happened. As I made the left turn out of my folks' subdivision onto Route 25A, in a desolate, woodsy area, I noticed an ice cream truck farther ahead on the highway. One of those trucks like "Good Humor" that parades around suburban neighborhoods playing jingles with jingle bells. This sight, combined with the sound of the bells, froze me in my tracks.

I had to stop the car and pull over. Another car screeched its brakes, skidded, then resumed control and swerved past me, sounding its horn and giving me "the finger." But I couldn't help it. I felt possessed.

This was June 1, 1976, just before twilight. The setting sun seemed white and cold like a big ball of snow on the horizon above a line of blue trees. Suddenly I ceased to be an adult and became a child again, a child four or five years old.

I was swimming in some kind of deja vu experience. That, at least, is how I rationalized it afterwards. The sight of the ice cream truck had brought back, in the way of classic Freudian analysis, a buried childhood trauma. Today I'm convinced this was nothing more than a "screen memory." But this is what I remembered:

I was four or five, an ice cream truck rolled up to our house where I lived with my parents, and I was lured away by its driver and placed onto the passenger seat of the cab. I made no protest, my mouth was filled with ice cream. I was self-possessed, perfectly content. So long as my mouth stayed full I didn't care what happened to me. The driver of the truck was a large man in a white overall, wearing glasses with dark lenses. He kept driving, bells ringing and merrily jingling, farther and farther away from my home. Finally he pulled into a deserted forest clearing, at which time I was removed from the passenger seat, put inside the refrigerated space of the truck where the ice cream pops are kept, and molested.

All this came flooding back to me as I sat behind the steering wheel, my eyes flooding with tears and my heart pounding a mile a minute.

I told myself this buried memory must account for a lot of the troubles I'd had growing up. In the mid-70s, we were just beginning to hear about child abuse, the sexual victimization of children. I counted myself one of them and, although some of the details seemed bizarre, I chalked it up to the nature of the child sex experience.

As the years went on, however, I began to doubt my own recollections of this event. For one thing, I couldn't believe that a sex criminal, no matter how deranged,

148

would climb into an ice cream truck freezer. I dunno, what do you think? I realize you don't pose as a sex crime expert but you're a man of the world, possibly of more than one world, right? So please give me some feedback if you'd be so kind.

Then two years ago I had another experience which made me doubt my sanity. I woke up about 6 a.m., a strange white light covering my room. I felt an intense chill but, even so, I was sweating. The walls looked like they'd been dipped in frost and reminded me of the inside of a huge refrigerator.

Although I can't explain why, I immediately knew that what had happened to me in my childhood had not been a case of sexual molestation, not in any ordinary sense anyway, but a violation by some alien presence. And this presence was again in my room. (MY WIFE DODIE, DID NOT FEEL THIS CHILL. SHE DID NOT EVEN WAKE UP.)

The impression of a powerful force of evil remained with me for days. I couldn't shake it.

I thought back to my mental picture of my molester. His eyes, hidden behind the almond-shaped lenses of his glasses; his white suit, which I had thought part of a uniform, suddenly reassembled itself into the protective garments of a lab technician.

The frost that had surrounded me that day, and on the night I spoke of two years ago, I now re-vision as being part of a much larger space than the confines of a Good Humor truck. Bigger than any bedroom too. These spaces were only the re-castings my mind had worked on the real space into which I was abducted, a space much vaster than I could comprehend

The molester's face didn't much resemble the face on the cover of your book *Communion*, although it shared the same blank black eyes and skinny lips, the elongated ears and the bulbous head. Also, some kind of shiny metal apparatus dangled from a belt around

149

his waist, which I misfigured as the kind of change dispenser ice-cream men wear. But it was not meant for dispensing change: that I know now. It contained some kind of battery or Geiger counter, buzzing and shirring and emitting electrical impulses I took for sexual ones.

-20-

LIZARD STRATEGY: APPEAR, THEN DISAPPEAR

Furiously, the coming apocalyps(o) began to syncopate my nerves. I wanted to re-vision a green green world where we all could ska harmoniously, but midnight abandoned my imagination. Would wit ever again grace the pages of this book? Would heresy ever again promp lyrics as compelling as those we danced to in The Lizard Club? Such questions staggered helplessly in my mind as drugs fell vicariously from the sky. Thus, too, fell I, back on devices old as Petronius used, namely cheap barroom chit-chat.

* * * * *

JEROME: I wish some creative lips would cream my jeans.
LEX: I wish fuliginous Egypt would fall from a banana slug as a colonic dollop.
DIET: I wish you'd quoted *ME* more in this scantless farrago.
ME: I wish this collaborative novel could flatten the endless permutations of racism, sexism, and anthropomorphism.
SEAN: Ya, and free us from the clutches of church, state, and capital too!

* * * * *

As usual, the other clubscene flowers hesitated (waiting, no doubt, for a fashion signal from their heresiarch), and unused signifiers twitched eagerly, anticipating some soon-to-blossom effervescence. Maddy took this opportunity to query Jerome on a subject that had long intrigued her.

> MADDY: I don't quite how to put this, but are you polysexual?
> JEROME: I sure am, honey, and Polly here wants a *cracker*!

Lex then employed an oxymoron, which had to be spanked minutes later for conduct unbecoming its morphemes. ("'Arroint thee witch,' the rump-fed runyon cried.") The jaded dwebes and twit-headed twerps standing around us were aghast.

"We *tried* to be good," one African gecko cried.

"Ya, and biology *tried* to recapitulate ontology too," I retorted. Then I thought again of Squirmy, hallucinating the magic of his eyes, his laugh, his nervous and unstable character. Were Squirmy's solipsistic balls still loitering about somewhere in Burma just waiting to be suckled? If only I could grab a moonbeam—like kids used to in fairytales—and bring everything to a happy conclusion. But all I could manage was to sneak off to the john, blow a boy from Brisbane, and return grinning stupidly—beyond philosophy, if not Kenneth Anger's demon mirror.

"Horseshit accepted the federal slushfund of her state-of-the-art career opportunity," Maddy was saying to Diet when I returned.

"I wish *God* or lesbians from Mars had been writing this instead of me," I protested. "At least then everything wouldn't have started stagnating so pathetically."

"But don't you see," Maddy rejoined. "It just depends on what *kind* of god you choose to be. Even if you're an atheist, or a Beat-Zen heretic, those are still beliefs—beliefs *you're* responsible for—so why not choose one you really dig?"

But already Maddy, Lex, Jerome, Diet, Sean, and all the rest were starting to fade—not because they *weren't* real, but because they were. For it's only the real that decays and dies, not the unreal.

> The troglodytes
> they let to grots
> the spheric ciphers sing.
> So war distended nets I draw
> this lizard drasil thing...

And like some faintly remembered tune from childhood, or the dream I'd had of Omewenne's song, I marvelled at how quickly we'd all changed. We danced, sang, drank and fucked, and what did we have to show for it? Not much. Chaos moved, then closed. Screw burned down. New clubs came and went. But the raving venues of our sexual and theological liberation had faded into oblivion. Yet though we didn't last as long as certain early heresies, our lives were not less glorious for that. We'd found freedom in the moment, in the cracks, and that was something. Better we now drift off, maybe to do nothing or to create something entirely new, before we become a "church."

So I walked out of The Lizard Club, as I'd walked out of The Saurian League, without looking back or saying goodbye. Not that I'd renounced my decadent, ambiguous homosaurian nature. Quite the contrary. But as Count Lesard once observed, "If you stay too long in one spot, someone will either nail you to a wall or slam you in a zoo."

And that I was determined to avoid.

153

-21-

FAMOUS LAST WORDS

(a pastiche of last lines from 101 of my favorite books)

Dear Mother:

Dim jerky stars are blowing away across a gleaming empty sky. Tonight I shall meditate upon that which I am. I'm like I was back then, really. Well, almost always... designing the elements of my own car crash. I have not come to since, and I never shall.

I am now discovering that reason, unable in the first place to prevent our misfortunes, is even less equal to consoling us for them. Was it for this piece of knowledge that I journeyed so far? Alone I cannot carry this burden of joy and doubt. You my double, my witness... there, lean over with me... let's look together... does it emit, deposit... as on the mirror we hold before the mouth of the dying... a fine mist? Who knows but that, on the lower frequencies, I speak for you. So, against you I will fling myself, unvanquished and unyielding!

(So it goes in the world. "Well, I'll have a cup of tea," a voice interrupts the words of what has already been said. But it is difficult for words to say that which it is their purpose to deny.)

Lord, how quickly it gets dark here. Night and the deafening racket of crickets again engulf the garden and the veranda, all around the house... leading to this page, this sentence, this full stop, by the old pen frequently and mechanically dipped into the blue-black ink. But let's return to the subject.

There are many things to be done towards the business of living, but I decided I don't no more know what to do than if I was just another lousy human being. Pity the unbeliever who would feign believe, or the galley-slave who goes to sea alone at night, beneath a firmament no longer lit by the consoling beacon-fires of the ancient hope. They're just waiting for you to try something stupid like that. But now each time I read your letter I feel confident again.

The supersensuality has lifted now, and no one will ever make me believe that the sacred wenches of Benares, or Plato's rooster, are images of God. This temple was built by neither Semiramis nor the Queen of Sheba, but they say that on its stones are engraved the principal secrets of Nicholas Flamel, more enigmatic even than those of Paracelsus. For instance, "An addition of information must fly," or "The care with which there is incredible justice and likeness, all this makes a magnificent asparagus, and also a fountain," or, "This isn't eternity, have I said that yet?" But, however passionate, sinning and rebellious the heart hidden in this tomb, the flowers growing over it peep serenely.

It was only after daybreak, after all the dancers had left, that Sir Stephen and the Commander, awakening Natalie, helped O to her feet, led her to the middle of the courtyard, unfastened her chain and removed her mask and, laying her back upon a table, possessed her. I saw no shadow of another departing from her. So it's not a question of suicide; it's only a question of beating a record.She was alone. The next day, I left the bathroom.

(O all these gold ribbons, blowing with the rhythm of

breathing, breathe in, breathe out, the light falls quite gently now, breasts heaving, red blood become milk! Beauty will be CONVULSIVE or it will not be at all.)

What then? I don't know. Who can tell? Surely the reader cannot be so stupid as not to remember what happened next.

P——— was sitting downcast and mumbling something incoherent and senseless. He was withered, wrinkled and loathsome of visage... like a gigantic whirligig beetle which has had the left half of its brain extracted. "You understand," said the old man. "People repeat what they've been told; a misfortune for instance, they say it's a testing time or just something you have to put up with, they don't look any further. But misfortune has no date. It does not arrive one day and fly away the next, it's there, it doesn't budge, we experience it or not according to unknown laws." That is what he tells me.

"Like a *lizard*!" he said; it was as if the shame of it must outlive him. "Forever," he said. He told Grace he'd rather just be effeminate. He only hopes his hat may not have given you a headache. And the dog, too, gave up then and lay down, his eyes bloodshot, his head flat.

The argument that next develops is one in which various explanations on widely different scales interact, forcing language to a new scale of discourse that includes all these possible conflicts—and the motivation behind them (e.g. *Why can't lizards go to heaven*?). Unfortunately, they agreed about nothing at all. I lingered, wondering how anyone could ever imagine unquiet slumbers for the sleepers in that quiet earth.

Then she saw him moving farther and farther away, farther and farther into the darkness until he was a pin point of light. As he caught his footing, his head fell back, and the Milky Way flowed down inside him with a roar. That was the last thing he ever saw. He did not stir. He was so tired. He died with a whimper. After the autopsy, all our medical experts rejected any

157

possibility of insanity. He was soon borne away by the waves and lost in darkness and distance. And wherever he may have disappeared to, I wish him luck.

Then I fled, my face in my hands. A plague of confusion has followed me ever since. No... it all happened. Go and see for yourself, if you don't believe me. We want no proofs; we ask none to believe us! Someday I shall write about all this in greater detail.

(So that is why music and dancing came from Guinea, God sent it there first—A way a lone a last a love a long the *lickety-lickety-lickety-split*—the tune was "My Heart's in the Highlands.")

In a little while I shall place these written pages in an empty oxygen cylinder and throw them into the deep. I leave it to be settled, by whomsoever it may concern, whether the tendancy of this work be altogether to recommend parental tyranny or reward filial piety. For me, it will be an act of piety for everything that lives is Holy ... and the dark and dank tarn at my feet will close sullenly and silently over the fragments....

...and among the forms in my dream are you, who like myself are many and no one. Because you thought you were special. Because I feel anxious to know... Because... (Her same eyes, her same mouth, open in surprise to see, at last, her long-cherished wish. We must have looked at each other like two blank crossword puzzles confronting themselves.) That was the end of us!

Then we walk out into the polyped street and in some miraculous manner are transformed into passersby. The miracle at last! The light went out; is going out. It is in the future that we must see our history.

Trust me.

God goes with thoughtless people.

Smell the flowers while you can.

A story like this can have no happy ending ...or can it?

Toward us, singing, came eleven little blind girls from the orphanage of Julius the Apostolic. For the first time they had done something out of love. Matter of fact, I think this was the youngest we ever felt. It was our best time. But we couldn't find a single mention in the press of this turning point in our lives.

Photo: Stan J. Maletic

Steve Abbott

A Bay Area critic, poet and novelist, Steve Abbott is also the author of five additional books, including *Holy Terror; View Askew: Postmodern Investigations; Lives of the Poets;* and *Skinny Trip to a Far Place.*. He served since 1979 as editor of *Poetry Flash* and *Soup* magazines.

Steve Abbott died of AIDS in December, 1992.